For my bea... , kind, smart daughter, Alexandria. One of the characters in this book, "Ria," is named after you. She is loving, kind, & generous, like you! Thank you for supporting me in my writing journey.

I love you to the moon and back!

Mom
6·22·2021

P.S. You got the VERY FIRST printed copy!

Civil

©2021, Julianna Lyn Oakes

ISBN: 978-1-09838-009-0

ISBN eBook: 978-1-09838-010-6

CIVIL

Julianna Lyn Oakes

— FOREWORD —

In 2018 a friend and I spent a well-deserved ladies' weekend at Glen Eyrie castle in Colorado Springs. Captivated by the immaculate castle and its period furnishings, and stunned by the surrounding landscape, my thoughts continued to drift. I found myself wondering what it might have been like for General Wynston Jamison Panton and his family to live in the grand Tudor castle nestled against the red rocks of the Rocky Mountain west during the late 1800s.

Upon returning home, I noticed a few strange balls of light in a couple of photographs taken during the weekend. My research did not turn up any suggestion that Glen Eyrie Castle might be haunted, and to be frank I've yet to see any evidence that hauntings are real, but still my imagination soared. Though I did not begin the process of writing *Civil* until two years after my visit to Glen Eyrie, the story itself marinated in the most active parts of my imagination for some time.

As a debut author, I am deeply indebted to my generous and talented friend, Holly Delants. She was the first reader and incredibly scrutinizing editor for the manuscript prior to its publication. In her words, "It is well-written and easy to follow. It is clever and compelling. It is unique. The characters were appealing with depth and personality, and I liked the way they developed. The recipes are a fun touch. I really enjoyed it. Civil is very uplifting and fitting for the world we live in today."

Finally, the love and encouragement from my husband and children to pursue my desire to write for enjoyment made *Civil* possible. I hope you will enjoy the characters, the mystery, and the incredible culinary delights that *Civil* has to offer!

— CHAPTER 1 —

Any Good Real Estate Agent Knows

The cool sting of snowflakes on her nose and cheeks and the sound of her skis gliding effortlessly through undisturbed powder were invigorating for Lena as silhouettes of fir, pine, and naked aspen trees obscured her peripheral vision like passing ghosts against the brilliant blue Colorado sky. She navigated the steep terrain skillfully, appreciating the crisp February afternoon. The private ski area at Elk Island Ranch offered the escape Lena had been craving for months. She leaned into the slope behind her, applied pressure to the upslope edges of her skis and eased to a graceful parallel stop.

Lena firmly planted her ski poles into the snow and gazed down at the 16,000 square foot lodge. Catering to elite and wealthy real estate clients certainly had its benefits! She wondered what her mother, a cotton mill worker, would have thought of a property so large and extravagant. Lena considered her humble beginnings as a small-town beauty queen from Cordele, Georgia where possum stew was a regular staple and poverty was something most folks had in common.

When Lena was 17 years old her widowed mother had taken a second job cleaning office buildings at night to help Lena afford clothing, make-up, and travel to the Miss Georgia pageant. Lena had felt lost in a sea of wealthy peroxide-blonde debutantes when she arrived at the pageant venue. No one expected the shy brunette with deep black eyes and a plain department store evening gown to place, much less win the title of Miss Georgia, but Lena's interview and passion for diversity and inclusive excellence made a lasting impression on the judges. Her interest in race relations was rooted in the fact that her great-great grandmother was a Black woman, the daughter of freed slaves who married a White man several years after the end of the Civil War. Though Lena's physical appearance did not suggest Black lineage, she had long embraced her unique heritage and was deeply troubled by the blatant racism she witnessed in rural Georgia.

The pageant scholarship made college possible for Lena, and she had been the first person in her family to earn a college degree. Following the death of their mother from brown lung disease caused by exposure to cotton dust while working at the mill, Lena paid for her younger sister, Gwyn, to attend culinary arts school. The cycle of poverty for Lena's family had finally been broken.

Intentionally single, independent, and smart, Lena loved her job as an agent for the luxury real estate firm, Chamberlain International Realty. The youngest agent and first woman promoted to vice president at the firm, Lena had grown accustomed to working with the rich, the famous, and the eccentric. She found humor in the challenge of maintaining an aloof and unimpressed demeanor with her clients and enjoyed the comfortable lifestyle her career afforded her. Lena had clients around the world, most of whom preferred to conduct their real estate communications and transactions through personal assistants.

A woodpecker making a ruckus in a nearby tree startled Lena, bringing her attention back to her present surroundings. Just an hour from the touristy Breckenridge and Steamboat Springs resorts, Elk Island Ranch was the year-round playground of David Oliver, an Australian singer-songwriter, and one of the world's best-selling recording artists. David had received six Grammy's and, most recently, had been named 36th on Rolling Stone Magazine's list of 100 most influential musicians of the rock and roll era.

Lena tugged her gloves off and placed them fingers-up on the handles of her ski poles. She reached into her jacket's inner pocket and removed the flask David's assistant had prepared for her - it was David's favorite ski treat, which he had named *The Kremmling* after the small town near Elk Island Ranch. Equal parts RumChata and peppermint schnapps, the sweet concoction warmed her throat as Lena reflected on how she met David.

Four years prior, a personal assistant named Ria had e-mailed the office to schedule a consultative appointment with Lena for a celebrity who was interested in purchasing a Colorado vacation property but wished to maintain a low profile. To Lena's surprise, the "celebrity" did not arrive at the Denver Chamberlain International Realty office with an assistant or a bodyguard. Dressed in jeans, a form-fitting white tee shirt and aviators, David Oliver had arrived in a blood red Corvette ZR1 convertible. His trademark golden hair had been pulled back in a man bun, windswept wisps of hair dangling gently against his strong, square jaw. He had been accompanied only by an affable English bulldog named Popeye who had promptly made himself comfortable on Lena's feet.

"I need a place where I can escape," David had said. "Something in the mountains with acreage – a lot of acreage. If the ideal property doesn't have an air strip, we need enough land to build one. My partner, Ben, and I have two boys. We want this to be a place where we can have a little normalcy and enjoy the outdoors – a place where we can fish, hike, snowshoe, and ski. A quiet place where I can write and record. We'd rather not be in a tourist-heavy area."

Lena had known just the place – Elk Island Ranch. With a listing price of $36 million, the 6,300-acre property featured a private air strip, massive log cabin style lodge with five bedrooms, 12 bathrooms and a majestic three-story log staircase. Next to the lodge was a separate entertaining saloon with a bar, dance floor, gaming tables, and a large garage for a car collection that could be converted to a recording studio. The property's private ski runs, trout-rich river, and hiking trails were accentuated by a chalet complete with a gourmet kitchen, bar, river stone fireplace, and sleeping quarters for twelve guests. The previous owner, a folk singer, had vanished mysteriously the prior year after taking off from the property in his Long EZ aircraft.

Despite rumors that the missing singer's ghost haunted the woods, David adored the property and purchased it on the condition that Lena personally teach him and his family to ski. He suspected the former owner had vanished voluntarily to escape the limelight and his wife, who was well known by music industry insiders as a sloppy drunk. In the four years since David purchased the property, Lena had received an annual invitation to visit and had developed a fondness for David, his family, Popeye the foot-warming dog, and David's assistant, Ria.

The rhythmic swoosh of skis approaching brought Lena out of her reminiscing. Lowering her ski goggles, she turned to see David approaching. With a mischievous grin he aimed a giant wave of white powder in her direction as he leaned upslope and came to an abrupt stop.

"Hey!" Lena exclaimed as she fastened the lid on her flask. "I swear, I should never have taught you to ski. You've become a real snow brat!"

"Sorry, Lena. Just getting in a run before dinner. Chef says carnitas and margaritas will be ready at 6:00, and I'm starving." David reached for Lena's flask and helped himself to a sip. "But since I've found you, I'd love to show you the old miner's cabin – that is, unless you're afraid you might see our resident ghost."

"What cabin?" Lena asked. David pointed up the small incline to his left. Through the trees, just beyond a large rock outcropping Lena could see the corner of what appeared to be an old log cabin. "I had no idea there was another structure on the property," she said. "I *really* love old buildings, and I don't believe in ghosts. Either do you. Can we go inside the cabin?"

David nodded. "Yeah. You up for a bit of a hike in your ski boots?" The two removed their skis and began the short uphill trek through the undisturbed knee-deep snow.

Just beyond the rocky outcropping and partially obscured by trees stood the remains of a small log cabin no more than 15 feet by 15 feet. The structure leaned slightly westward, a likely result of the wind, but it appeared to be in fair condition. The chinking between the logs was mostly intact, and a stone chimney peeked from the top of the sagging pine-shingled roof. Two square wood-framed windows provided a glimpse into the dark interior. David gave the splintered wood door a shove with his shoulder. With a creak that reminded Lena of something out of a horror movie, the door opened just enough to permit David to squeeze through.

Lena followed slowly, stepping only a few feet into the cabin. While she adored history and old homes more than just about anything, deserted mining cabins in the middle of nowhere seemed oddly creepy to her. Adjusting to the darkness of the room, Lena squeezed her eyes shut and then surveyed the inside of the cabin.

A small stone fireplace with an iron pot inside of it caught her attention. On the hearth lay an old iron skillet and the feathery remains of a long-dead bird. A warped and rusted metal gold pan was propped up against the wall on a crude wooden shelf; Lena thought it surely must have been used to pan for gold in the Colorado River, which ran by the bottom of the hill. She made a mental note to do some research about whether the gold industry had impacted the area during the gold rush.

The three-legged remnant of a hand-made wooden chair leaned lazily in a corner under a warped wooden window, which was partially obscured by the tattered remains of an old white lace curtain. A lover of history, Lena wondered who might have lived here. She imagined it must not have been a solitary miner, because lace curtains were a sure sign of female presence.

David stood to Lena's left; his brows furrowed as he squinted at something on the floor. He pulled off his ski gloves and removed his cell phone from his coat pocket. "Yummy," he said quietly, aiming the phone's flashlight downward near his feet. Lena's eyes followed the light from David's phone to the floor and what appeared to be an old blood stain and a few small bones.

"Yuck! Either something got eaten there or…" Lena didn't finish her sentence. The sound of slow, heavy footsteps in the snow outside the cabin made her freeze in fear. She reached forward and grabbed David's elbow in a panic. Meeting his eyes, she was surprised to see that David was smiling at her. Quietly, he raised his left hand and pointed behind her to the partially open cabin door.

Fearing of what might be behind her, Lena turned slowly and saw something move. There stood a massive bull elk easily five feet high and nine feet long with large, heavy antlers. Surprised, Lena let out a high-pitched scream, reeled backward and, with all her weight, forced the cabin door shut.

David doubled over, laughing heartily, as the sound of the startled elk's footsteps faded in the distance. "That was *not* funny!" Lena exclaimed as she smacked him in the head with her glove. David's laughter transformed into an unflattering snort and the two laughed until they cried.

"We see that great big moose around from time to time" Ben said when he finally caught his breath. "Ben has named him Bullwinkle." David wiped his eyes and pulled the heavy cabin door open. "Come on, city girl - you've scared away all the wildlife! The sun is setting, so we had better hurry down the hill. Ria should be back from town by now, and we should clean up before dinner. Besides, we don't want to keep Ben and the boys waiting – *hangry* is never a good thing." Still recovering from fright, Lena finished off the contents of her flask as the pair hiked back to their skis and returned to the lodge.

The air in the lodge dining room was heavy with the slightly spicy, citrusy smell of slow-cooked carnitas. David's chef had prepared homemade tortillas, guacamole, and salsa. Lena marveled at the ornately carved buffet table, on which even the shredded lettuce and diced tomatoes were artfully displayed. Cucumber-infused water replenished her slope-tired muscles, and blood orange margaritas helped to liven the meal-time dialogue.

After dinner David, Lena, Ben, and Ria retired to the great room. The massive antler chandelier and fire in the three-story river rock fireplace cast a warm glow over the friends as they sipped iced blood orange margaritas. Popeye dropped a tennis ball in Ben's lap and curled up on Lena's feet. Lena had never owned a dog and her busy lifestyle certainly would not permit her to have one, but chubby, endearing Popeye had earned a place in her heart – and on her feet.

"Lena, I hope you don't mind, but there is a real estate matter that Ria needs your help with. Before we discuss details, I need to ask you to try to have an open mind." David took a deep breath and exchanged a nervous glance with Ria before continuing. "I don't know what I'd do without Ria. She is one heck of a personal assistant and nanny to the boys, but she is much more than that. She is also one of our dearest friends. Ria was married to Ben's childhood best friend, James Panton."

Seated in a love seat beside Ben, Ria raised her head and met Lena's eyes as a tear slipped silently down her cheek. Concerned, Lena watched as, grasping Ben's hand, Ria drew a ragged breath. "I know that I will never love again as deeply as I loved James. He was my everything, and he was a wonderful father to our daughter, Melissa. Unfortunately, he passed away unexpectedly from a heart attack just before Thanksgiving." Ria closed her eyes and placed a hand over her mouth momentarily before continuing. "Melissa is grown now; her husband is a Lieutenant Colonel in the Air Force stationed in Japan. That leaves me to tend to the estate, which is rather complicated, in many ways."

"Oh, Ria. I'm so sorry," Lena said, watching as Ria brushed a lock of wavy, shoulder-length strawberry blonde hair behind her ear and dabbed at her emerald green eyes with a tissue. Somehow Ria appeared older than she had before, and tired. Lena wondered how much of an estate someone who worked as a nanny and personal assistant could possibly have.

Ben patted Ria's knee gently. He blinked away accumulated tears from his own eyes and cleared his throat. "Lena, I know you love old homes. You are also a bit of a history buff, aren't you?" Lena nodded. "Perhaps you have read about General Wynston Jamison Panton, the founder of Colorado Springs." Again, Lena nodded, realizing that the Panton surname must be the connection to Ria's husband. "Wynston Jamison Panton was James' great-great-grandfather. The family home, Glen Eyrie Castle, has been handed down through the generations in James' family. James was the last living male in the Panton family."

Stunned, Lena set her margarita glass on the granite-topped coffee table in front of her. She vaguely remembered reading about Glen Eyrie Castle in an issue of *Architectural Digest* several years ago. The English Tudor-style castle was near Garden of the Gods Park on the north side of Colorado Springs, though that was all she really remembered. "Ria," Lena said softly, "you own Glen Eyrie Castle?"

Ria shook her head. "No. James owned it – my name was never on the deed. But he left everything to me. We have always lived in the carriage house on the property; it was converted to a home by James' parents for us as a wedding gift. We raised Melissa there. James' parents lived in the castle until 1994 when we moved them to a nursing facility in Colorado Springs, but they are both gone now. We've used the castle for weddings and special occasions over the years, but… well, it just wasn't a good place for us to live or raise a child, for many reasons." The room filled with an awkward silence as Ria's gaze settled on the fire.

"The property is just over 600 acres, Lena. The castle was the General's dream home, which he built for his wife. Her name was Marie, but apparently the General always called her 'Queenie.' Thus, a castle, I suppose." Ria managed a half smile before continuing. "It has 67 rooms, two towers, a great hall, and 24 fireplaces. It really is grand – it is furnished with original pieces from England dating back to the 1700s. The castle looks like something you would expect to see in England, and the family has spared no expense in maintaining the castle and the grounds. It is a time capsule of sorts. My favorite piece is a medieval Italian iron knight that stands just inside the entrance."

Ria closed her eyes, laid her head on Ben's shoulder, and sighed softly. "I'm all alone now. The property and the castle – even the carriage house, frankly – are just too much for me to keep up. I suppose it could be a museum or events facility, but I really don't know what to do. What I do know is that it should be preserved. Lena, please help me figure out what to do."

Lena stared blankly at Ria. Why would a woman of such means work as a personal assistant and nanny for a famous rock star? Why wouldn't she want to keep the castle? Why live in a carriage house when you could opt to live in a castle? Lena's mind raced. Swallowing the last of her margarita Lena glanced at David, who was glaring at Ben with raised eyebrows as if to prompt him to say more. Ben shifted nervously, sighed, and muttered something under his breath. He stood up and paced in front of the fire for several minutes before sitting on the coffee table facing Lena.

"James grew up in the castle," he said. Placing his elbows on his knees and resting his chin on clasped hands, Ben looked at her as if trying to discern whether he should share more. "I spent a lot of time there as a kid because James was my best friend. The place is amazing, Lena. But… God, you're going to think I'm nuts." Ben ran both hands though his hair and lowered his head. Without looking up he whispered, "Lena, the place is haunted."

Lena wondered if Ben had lost his mind and could not help but blink her eyes in disbelief. She had always understood Ben as a bit of a modern-day hippie, and not just because of his long hair and affinity for wearing Birkenstock sandals year-round. Ben was a believer in auras and crystals and many other things that Lena categorized as nothing short of silly. Half Cherokee, Ben claimed to be a medicine man. Of course, he also claimed to be a Druid priest. A notable poet, Ben brought unique perspectives to any conversation, but *ghosts*?

Noting the skeptical expression on Lena's face, Ben cleared his throat nervously and asked, "Do realtors legally have to disclose it if a property is haunted? The place could be hard to sell, Lena. *Really* hard to sell."

Realizing she was staring at Ben with a great deal of skepticism, Lena forced her gaze to Ria who nodded slightly. "It's true, Lena." Ria folded her hands nervously in her lap and looked down. "The ghosts are the reason I couldn't live in the castle. James grew up in the place, so he was used to it, but I have always found the castle to be a terrifying place. Most of the time it is just strange sounds and smells, which I could probably live with. But objects move on their own and I have seen several spirits."

Lena folded her arms over her chest and raised an unconvinced eyebrow, but Ria continued, "The night we brought Melissa home from the hospital I saw a middle-aged brunette woman in a long blue dress leaning over her crib. She had her hair in a fancy twist with curls sort of hanging around her face. When I screamed the woman disappeared into thin air! James tried to convince me I was exhausted from labor and delivery and hadn't seen anything at all, but I know what I saw."

Ria finished her margarita, then stood slowly and strode to the fireplace, tugging at the hem of her heavy wool cardigan. "James was a wonderful man, Lena," Ria said, "but he wouldn't leave the place no matter how much I begged. With Melissa away at boarding school and James traveling frequently, I was too scared to be at the property alone. So about five years ago when David and Ben mentioned they were looking for help with the boys and David's schedule, I convinced them to hire me. It gave me a reason to be away from Glen Eyrie and, frankly, the position probably saved my sanity."

David rose from his chair and picked up the pitcher of margaritas. He refilled Ria's glass, then handed the pitcher to Ben. David sat down next to Lena and looked at her seriously. "I didn't believe it myself until I stayed there, but sure as shit… the place is spooky. I heard footsteps walking back and forth in the hall outside my room all night long. Not heavy footsteps that might belong to a man – light footsteps that sounded like a woman in high heels. In the middle of the night someone pounded the hell out of the door to my room, but when I opened the door no one was in the hall. James used to claim that the old suit of armor on the main floor was haunted, too. He said it would move around the first floor!"

Lena crossed her arms and raised an eyebrow at David, who proclaimed, "Lena, I'm telling the truth. I *promise!*"

A property like Glen Eyrie Castle would be a unique opportunity, so Lena knew she had to carefully balance respect for her friends with her own pragmatic beliefs. "Look, I don't mean any disrespect, but there is no such thing as ghosts. I may be interested in helping you sell the castle if that's what you really want to do, Ria. But I'd need to check the place out and have it appraised before I commit to anything."

"Thank you, Lena. I would be grateful." From the pocket of her sweater Ria pulled a small drawstring leather pouch. "David has a short tour starting in 10 days. Ben and the boys and I will be joining him, so we'll all be traveling until around the first of March," Ria said as she handed the pouch to Lena.

"These are keys to the castle and carriage house. Go down for a visit while we are on tour with David, but please do not go alone. Take some friends and stay a few days in the castle, Lena. Get to know the place. Get to know the General. Just text me when you can make it. I'll leave some information for you with the guard at the security gate."

Chapter One Recipes

The Kremmling – An Après Ski Delight

1. In a zip-top sandwich bag, use a meat cleaver or hammer to smash two candy canes into tiny bits. Pour mixture onto a sheet of wax paper or foil and distribute evenly.

2. Add enough water to a small plate that it stands in a puddle slightly wider than the rim of your martini glass.

3. Gently dip the rim of the martini glass into the water so that it coats just the rim, then dip the rim into the candy cane bits to rim the glass.

4. In a cocktail shaker (or glass), mix equal parts RumChata and peppermint schnapps. Add ice and shake (or stir) well.

5. Pour beverage into rimmed martini glasses and enjoy!

Colorado Carnitas

3-4 lb. boneless pork (shoulder or butt) roast
Zest of one orange
1 Mexican (pure cane sugar) bottled Coke
4 cloves minced garlic
3/4 large white or yellow onion (finely chopped)
1 jalapeno (seeded and finely chopped)
1 cinnamon stick
2 bay leaves
1 T. sugar
2 t. crushed dried oregano
1 t. crushed red pepper flakes
¼ t. ground cloves
¼ t. cumin

～

1 ½ t. salt

1 t. pepper

Chopped fresh cilantro for garnish

Salsa for garnish

Trim any thick fat from the surface of the roast, cut meat into 1-inch cubes, and place in a large pot on the stove top. Add enough water to cover the meat by at least an inch, then add all ingredients except the salt, pepper, cilantro, and salsa. Stir well.

Bring pot to a boil, then reduce to simmer uncovered for 90 minutes until the pork is very tender, adding more water periodically to keep the meat covered. When meat is tender add the salt and pepper, stir well, then continue to simmer uncovered until the water is evaporated (approximately 30 – 45 minutes).

Remove bay leaves and cinnamon stick. Shred meat using an electric mixer or two forks, and lay meat on a foil-lined cookie sheet. Place in the oven under broiler for five minutes until meat begins to crisp (for crispier meat, broil up to five minutes longer).

Serve on warm tortillas with salsa and cilantro garnish, sour cream, and guacamole.

Blood Orange Mountain Margaritas

> 2 c. Santo Mezquila Tequila by Sammy Hagar
>> OR Don Julio Blanco Tequila
>
> 2 c. blood orange juice
>
> ½ c. Cointreau
>
> 1 c. lime juice
>
> 2 t. pure vanilla extract
>
> 4+ T. agave nectar (sweeten to taste)

Blend ingredients in blender for 15 seconds. Pour over ice into prepared margarita glasses.

TIPS:

1. Like it sweet? Try rimming your glasses with Penzey's Vanilla Sugar!

2. Want it pretty? Use a channel zester to make curled strips of orange zest to place in your glasses.

— CHAPTER 2 —

Bourbon and Bravado

The daughter of immigrants from Cuba, Lena's student intern Jasmyn Diaz was pursuing a double major in business and history at a nearby private university. As an outstanding high school student, Jasmyn had received a first-generation scholars award that covered her tuition, books, and fees at the University of Denver. Jasmyn's father owned a liquor store not far from Lena's condo in Cherry Creek, and her mother operated a popular food truck selling Cuban food on Federal Boulevard near the Denver Broncos football stadium. Jasmyn's paid internship with Chamberlain International Realty afforded the family just enough money for Jasmyn to live on campus.

Exceptionally bright and exuberant, Jasmyn adored Lena and had quickly adopted her as a professional role model. Jasmyn's career aspiration was to purchase and restore historic homes eligible for the National Register of Historic Places, so she had been the perfect person to research General Panton and Glen Eyrie Castle for Lena. Jasmyn's brown eyes glistened with excitement as she clutched a manila folder to her chest and plopped herself into a chair facing Lena's desk.

"Lena, do you *know* who Wynston Jamison Panton was? I mean, yes, he founded Colorado Springs and Manitou Springs, provided funding to build Colorado College, and co-founded the Rio Grande railroad. But get this…" Jasmyn leaned forward eagerly, her brown eyes sparkling with excitement. "After his service in the Civil War, the dude actually donated some of his personal fortune to provide education for freed former slaves! Later he built a hospital in Colorado Springs for tuberculosis patients. During his lifetime, the guy donated what is equivalent to $112 million in today's money. He was *totally* a bad ass warrior for social justice!"

"We do not use the words *dude* or *ass* in the workplace, Jasmyn." Lena scolded as she smiled at the young woman. It occurred to her that the millennial generation's open mindedness, social justice focus, and hippie-ish pursuit of equity and peace might just change sociocultural norms in the United States for the better. Jasmyn was energetic, smart, and ambitious; she reminded Lena of her younger self, and Lena felt a special fondness for the young intern.

"You really want to go, don't you? I should warn you that the owner claims the place is haunted, so it might be scary."

Jasmyn nodded eagerly. "Yes! *Duh!* What I do outside of my work hours is my decision, so we can call this a personal trip or time off – no liability to the agency. Besides, I am almost 22 years old, so it's not like I'm a child. This will be good experience for me! Pleeeaaase, Lena? Los fantasmas no me asustan!"

"Huh? What the heck does *that* mean?" Lena asked, raising one eyebrow. From time-to-time Jasmyn spoke in Spanish even though she knew Lena could not understand it, and Lena wondered whether it was intentional or a subconscious tendency for bilingual persons.

Jasmyn winked at Lena, smiled mischievously, and replied "I ain't afraid of no ghost." She handed the folder to Lena. "Here's the research on General Panton and Glen Eyrie. It is probably more than you wanted, but the history was fascinating. When do we go?"

Lena chuckled at Jasmyn's reference to the Ghost Busters movie. "Let me reach out to the owner. I have an appraiser who is available late in the morning on Monday, so I am thinking Friday afternoon through midday Monday. I will let you know. Why don't you head back to campus before this storm gets any worse? I promise to bring you up to speed tomorrow."

With an eye on the increasingly heavy snow falling outside her office window, Lena packed up her briefcase, changed into snow boots, and donned a knee-length waterproof down coat. She wrapped a scarf around her neck, pulled the hood snugly over her head, and embarked on the short, snowy walk to the light rail station a block away.

Normally the light rail commute was an opportunity for Lena to look over contracts or engage in some people-watching. The diverse Denver community never failed to disappoint when Lena was in the mood to simply observe humanity during her daily commute. A myriad of smartly bundled evening commute passengers joined Lena at the light rail station. When her train arrived, she boarded and settled into an open seat next to a heavily bearded gentleman who smelled faintly of whiskey and cherry tobacco.

The ride from the agency to her condo at 1st Avenue and Fillmore Street in Cherry Creek would be a good time to read the research Jasmyn had provided. Removing her mittens, she fumbled through her black leather laptop bag and removed Jasmyn's folder of research on General Panton and Glen Eyrie Castle.

Born in 1836 and raised in a Quaker community, Wynston Jamison Panton married his wife Marie, whom he lovingly called "Queenie" in 1870. Panton served in the American Civil War; he received a Medal of Honor and was promoted to Brevet Brigadier General during the conflict. He was awarded the Medal of honor because, even though he had less than 200 men under his leadership, he "… attacked and defeated a superior force of the enemy, capturing their fieldpiece and about 100 prisoners without losing a man."

After the war was over, Panton personally funded education for a number of freed slaves. He led several profitable business ventures, including construction of the Kansas Pacific Railway and Denver/Rio Grande Railways, which later became known as Union Pacific Railways. Successful in establishing several rail-related businesses, Panton later co-founded what would become the city of Colorado Springs, and individually founded the nearby resort town of Manitou Springs.

In 1871 Panton built for his bride an elaborate home which he named "Glen Eyrie" (Scottish for "Valley of the Eagle's Nest"). Following expansions completed in 1903, Panton's Tudor-style mansion became known as Glen Eyrie Castle. Despite Queenie's fragile health she and the General had three daughters: Ruby, Flora, and Evalynn. Queenie passed away after a series of heart attacks in 1896..

After retiring, General Panton became a dedicated philanthropist, donating more than $4.5 million ($118 million current equivalent) to community-serving causes. He was a founding donor for Colorado College, built a tuberculosis hospital, and provided land and funding to build churches, parks, libraries, and the Colorado School for the Deaf and Blind in the Colorado Springs region. Tragically, a horseback riding accident in 1904 left General Wynston Jamison Panton paralyzed.

Panton drew his last breath in March 1909; on that day the bustling, picturesque city of Colorado Springs lowered its flags to half-staff. The mayor proclaimed Panton a philanthropist and friend of the community whose life's evident passion was blessing others. The Colorado Springs Gazette described General Panton as "an ardent pacifist, humanitarian and champion of preserving wildlands at a time when conservation was almost unheard of."

Wynston and his beloved wife, Marie "Queenie" Panton are buried at Evergreen National Cemetery in Colorado Springs.

Sources:

1. *"Panton, Wynston J., Civil War Medal of Honor recipient". American Civil War website. 2020-02-18. Retrieved February 18, 2020.*

2. *https://en.wikipedia.org/wiki/Wynston_Jamison_Panton*

3. *Dave Philipps (March 8, 2009). "Panton: A Founder, A Father Figure". The Gazette. Colorado Springs, Colorado.*

Lena arrived home in time to watch the sun set over the Rocky Mountains from her west-facing living room on the 6th floor of the high-end condominium complex. She turned on the gas fireplace and prepared a large pot of her grandmother's recipe for savory chicken and dumplings for dinner. The recipe had been adapted by Lena's mother over the years, and Lena had made her own adjustments as well, but it was the perfect dinner for snowy Colorado evenings as far as Lena was concerned. The rich broth and tender dumplings reminded Lena of her childhood and simpler days in Cordele, Georgia. She poured a bowl for herself, leaving the rest to cool so she could put individual servings in the freezer.

Ah, the perfect pairing, she thought as she poured a generous glass of Mourvèdre. Savoring the wine's earthy smell and dry, gamey notes she turned out the lights and settled on the living room floor in front of the fireplace, using the hearth as a table. She wondered what varieties of wine might be in the wine cellar at Glen Eyrie castle that Ria had mentioned. Chewing thoughtfully on a dumpling, she studied the photograph of Glen Eyrie Castle that Jasmyn had provided in her research.

Lena had always adored the architectural detail and history of old homes. It seemed to her that aesthetic detail and careful craftsmanship might be lost arts. Constructed of red stone, Lena found Glen Eyrie Castle to be both grandiose and rustic at the same time. The castle could be an inn, a library, or a museum just as easily as it could be a residence, she thought. She made a quick note to call the Colorado Springs City Council office in the morning to see if they might know of any needs or potential buyers for the old place.

Gazing occasionally into the fire while savoring a second glass of wine, Lena studied the photo of General Panton in Jasmyn's packet and realized that it seemed oddly familiar and comforting to her – almost as if she had taken it herself or gazed upon it a thousand times. Running her fingers over the General's jawline in the photo, she pondered the idea that dead people might return to Earth as spirits. Prior to Ria's declaration that Glen Eyrie was haunted, Lena had thought the woman to be a competent, practical individual. But ghosts?

Lena opened her laptop and logged on to check the Colorado Real Estate Manual. She was not surprised to learn that the state of Colorado's stigmatized property disclosure laws did not have guidelines pertaining to alleged paranormal activity associated with a residential dwelling.

3.1.13 Facts with the potential to elicit psychological impact or stigma, such as historical events, deaths, or tragedies that have occurred in a dwelling or on a property are not required to be disclosed unless a potential buyer specifically asks.

3.1.14 Federal case law suggests that any disclosure by a real estate agent of information deemed to be of a sensitive nature to potential buyers without the seller's permission may constitute a breach of ethics.

Lena closed her laptop and savored another sip of wine as she pondered whether public knowledge of a supposed haunting would help or hurt efforts to sell Glen Eyrie Castle for the highest possible amount.

A sudden surge from the gas fireplace tore Lena abruptly from her thoughts. The flames, higher and hotter than normal, seemed to take the shape of a face, but as quickly as Lena's mind registered the face it disappeared. She reeled backwards, catching her breath sharply. A strange, high-pitched shrieking sound emerged from the flames, prompting Lena to spring to her feet and turn off the switch to the fireplace.

Boy, that wine really packed a punch, she thought, laughing nervously at herself as she fumbled in the dark for a light switch. Her heart pounded heavily as she walked to the kitchen to retrieve her cell phone. Hands shaking, she found the contact listing in her phone for Frank, the condominium complex's resident handy man.

"Hello, this is Frank."

"Hi Frank, this is Lena Thomas in unit 612. I'm really glad you answered." Her voice was shaky.

"Everything alright, Miss Thomas?"

"Um yes, but I think I have a gas problem. My fireplace just had a… a surge or something. The flames got bigger, and then it made a loud sound.

Scared me to death. I turned it off, and I know it is after hours, but would you mind coming up to check it out for me, please?"

"Probably just a bad blower. Leave the fireplace off, okay? I'll be up in just a few minutes."

Glancing back toward the living room, Lena took in a deep breath through her nose and released it slowly through her mouth. The face in the flames must have been an odd coincidence caused by a malfunction with the fireplace. She prided herself for being a pragmatic and sensible person, yet she could not shake the uneasy feeling that someone was in the room with her. Too much wine and talk of ghosts, she supposed. Determined to ignore her sense of unease Lena refilled her wine glass, turned on some light jazz, put individual helpings of chicken and dumplings in the freezer, and loaded the dishwasher.

When the handy man arrived, Lena was grateful not to be alone. He confirmed that the fireplace needed a new blower and promised to return in a few days to make the repair. She thanked him again for coming by after hours and offered him an individual serving of chicken and dumplings to take home. Frank accepted the meal and joked that he would be sure to schedule the fireplace blower repair around dinnertime.

Outside the wind began to howl and large snowflakes danced gently in the city lights. Up to seven inches of snow was expected to fall overnight. Lena pulled an extra blanket from the hall closet and turned the thermostat up to 68 degrees. Then she washed her face, took two over-the-counter sleeping pills, and headed to bed. Her eyelids were heavy as she burrowed into the comforting weight of the blankets and imagined what Glen Eyrie Castle might look like inside.

Just as sleep began to overtake her, Lena thought she heard the faintest voice whisper, *"Seleeeena, come home."* She opened her eyes wearily and looked around the room. Deciding she had not really heard anything at all, Lena made a mental note to sip more slowly next time she had this particular wine, which had been a gift from a friend. Seeing a face in the fireplace flames must have been a result of a little too much wine, and she convinced herself that taking two over-the-counter sleeping aids after drinking probably caused the auditory hallucination. She had not actually heard a voice. Besides, no one had called her Selena since before her mother passed away.

Lena turned on her white noise machine and finally drifted to sleep. She dreamt she was walking through an aspen grove among short green shrubs that bore delicate, spiky red flowers. She could feel the warmth of the sun on her skin and smell the faint scent of pine. In the distance a deer and two twin fawns grazed in a misty meadow.

Ding! The sound of an incoming text message interrupted Lena's pleasant dream just before dawn. Chamberlain International Realty's Denver Office would be closed for the day due to accumulated snow and ice. Employees were encouraged to work from home to the extent their responsibilities permitted. Typical of Colorado's erratic weather patterns the Denver forecast called for a high of 55 degrees, so Lena knew the roads and sidewalks would be clear by afternoon. Enjoying the warmth of her blankets she decided to stay in bed for a while.

Lena called her sister Gwyn, whom she frequently invited to accompany her on trips. She knew Gwyn would love the idea of a castle, especially one with a substantial wine collection. Though naturally brunette like her sister, Gwyn wore her wavy shoulder-length hair in a deep auburn color. While Lena was introverted, athletic, and slender, Gwyn was chatty. She was also curvy and buxom, attributes developed during her career as a professional chef. The two sisters had always been close, even during their tumultuous teen years, and their bond had become stronger after the death of their mother. Lena had begun inviting Gwyn to tag along on occasional business trips to ensure that Gwyn did not lack emotional support following her fiancé's tragic death in a motorcycle accident.

Lena also called Kacie, her best friend from college, to invite her to enjoy the long weekend at Glen Eyrie castle, too. Blonde with blue eyes and a light smattering of freckles, Kacie was dramatic, boisterous, and dripping with southern charm. She had been raised in rural Kentucky where her family bred champion racehorses. She and Lena had met in graduate school at the University of Colorado in Boulder and become fast friends. Kacie always looked forward to adventures with Lena. A nurse by training, Kacie owned and operated a home health care company specializing in professional athletics. In fact, her ex-husband was a pitcher for the Colorado Rockies baseball team whom she had initially met as a client.

Both Gwyn and Kacie agreed to join Lena and Jasmyn for a long weekend at Glen Eyrie Castle. Gwyn promised to plan dinners worthy of royalty for the three nights at the castle, and Kacie offered to drive to Colorado Springs with Gwyn so they could stop and do grocery shopping on the way. With the guests committed to a castle adventure, Lena sent a text to Ria.

> Hi, Ria. My sister, a friend, and my real estate intern are excited to visit Glen Eyrie with me. I know it is short notice, but is Friday through Monday OK with you? Appraiser available Monday afternoon. Lena

> Yes, of course. Sounds like a great ladies' weekend! I'll have the heat turned up for you on Thursday evening. You have a set of keys – I will leave a note for you at the security gate. Flour, sugar, spices, and coffee in the main house kitchen, but that's about it.

> Thanks! My sister is a chef, so we will be fine. 😊

After confirming an 11:00 a.m. appointment with the appraiser for Monday, Lena called Jasmyn. They agreed to leave the office at noon on Friday and drive together to Glen Eyrie. Kacie planned to catch a ride with Gwyn to Colorado Springs; the two planned to arrive late afternoon after picking up groceries for the weekend. The schedule would give Lena and Jasmyn just enough time to tour the castle and form an honest opinion about its condition and market potential.

Rather than take the light rail to work that Friday as she preferred to do, Lena loaded her travel bag and briefcase into the back of her silver Range Rover and headed for the Chamberlain International Realty office in downtown Denver. Parking downtown was a headache when it came to finding available spots, but it was necessary from time to time. Once she had parked the car, Lena enjoyed the crisp, two-block walk from her parking spot to the office.

In front of the realty office, she stopped at her favorite coffee truck where she bought a latte for herself as well as coffees and toasted bagels with cream cheese for two homeless men huddled together in sleeping bags; she had seen them when she passed by the alley. As a child, Lena had benefitted from the generosity of Mr. Gerardy, a local baker who would give her day-old bread for her family in exchange for sweeping his shop. She had last spoken with Mr. Gerardy when she was home for her mother's funeral.

"Always share your treasure with the poor and the marginalized, Lena," he had said as he hugged her. Lena had promised to honor his generosity by paying it forward someday.

"Goodness, Lena Thomas. You really are one hell of a good person," said a woman's voice to her left as she exited the alley. There, leaning against the corner of the building was Jasmyn, hand resting in the extended handle of a large, bright purple roller suitcase with teal and brown owls on it.

"Always share your treasure with the poor and the marginalized, Jasmyn," Lena replied. Noticing the enormity of the intern's suitcase, Lena furrowed her brow. "It is a weekend trip, Jasmyn – not an international voyage. What in the world is in that huge suitcase?"

"All of the essentials, plus some recording equipment and a night vision camera and tripod I borrowed from a friend. If there are really any ghosts at the castle, I want proof." Jasmyn flashed a dimpled smile. "Oh, and my dad said to give you this as a thank you for everything you've done for me. You know my family owns a liquor store over in Cherry Creek, right? This is a bottle of Blanton's bourbon – it is supposed to be really good." She handed Lena a brown paper bag with a bottle in it.

"Mmmm… thank you!" Lena replied. "I can tell this is going to be a very interesting weekend!"

At midday Lena and Jasmyn left the office and departed for Colorado Springs. They stopped halfway to their destination in the quaint town of Castle Rock for gas. Lena adored the town for its boutique shops, rocky buttes, and well-kept hiking trails. Settlers had arrived in Castle Rock during the 1870s, lured by the gold rush and the rail industry. Midway between Denver and Colorado Springs, the town offered great appeal to outdoor enthusiasts, foodies, and golf lovers.

At Jasmyn's insistence, Lena agreed to stop for lunch at a locally owned restaurant named *Crave*. Owned by a Colorado couple who met and fell in love while students at Cherry Creek high school, *Crave* was legendary among Colorado residents for its commitment to serving only 100% Colorado-raised meat and its outlandish culinary approaches to the great American burger. From coffee-dusted onion strings and tempura-fried cream cheese to candied bacon and peanut butter, the restaurant's unique burger options had Jasmyn conflicted about what to order.

"I can feel my waistline expanding just looking at this menu!" Lena exclaimed. Though she chose a practical salad for lunch, Lena caved to the tempting menu by also ordering the *Millionaire* milkshake, which was made with coffee liqueur, Irish cream, and hazelnut liqueur. Lena watched in amazement as Jasmyn eagerly devoured the entirety of *The Luther Burger*, which consisted of a beef patty, fried egg, candied bacon, and cheese smooshed between two glazed donuts. *Someday Jasmyn's metabolism will catch up with her*, Lena thought enviously as she picked at her Cobb salad.

It was just after 2:00 when they pulled off the interstate onto Garden of the Gods Road and headed west. Five minutes later they approached the iron gated entrance to Glen Eyrie. After checking her identification, the guard at the entry gate handed Lena an envelope and opened the gate for her. Lena handed the envelope to Jasmyn, who read the note from Ria aloud while Lena slowly navigated the narrow dirt drive to the castle.

Dear Lena:

There is a laundry facility in the castle cellar by the wine room. Please help yourself to some wine (Lord knows there is plenty of it). Every room in the castle has at least one hurricane lamp or candle and a lighter (flashlight and cell phone batteries are worthless here). If you need anything, you can call my handy man, Calvin. His number is on the refrigerator in the kitchen at the carriage house along with the numbers of a few local friends.

Wireless Network: PantonFam
Username: MyMelissa
Password: JamesNRia

Here are some tidbits about the castle to share with your guests.

1. *Just inside the main entrance to the castle stands an authentic 16th century Italian knight suit of armor. None of us has ever witnessed it move, but it really does move time to time and the face shield opens and closes occasionally without explanation.*

2. *Several family members and guests have seen the General's ghost over the years. His daughters (James' great aunts) even claimed that he would leave them occasional gifts from the forest years after his death. Things like flowers and pinecones.*

3. *We often hear footsteps in the upstairs hall where the larger bedrooms are– not heavy footsteps, but light, feminine footsteps. Sometimes the lights flicker at the same time.*

4. *I believe the brunette woman in the long blue dress who I saw leaning over Melissa's crib is Queenie, the General's wife (there is a portrait of her in the dining room). Melissa saw her several times when she was younger but remembers her as a real person with whom she had full conversations.*

5. *It is fairly common to hear horses near the carriage house,
   though there haven't been horses on the property for several
   years.*

*Have fun. Text me when you leave, and I will have our maid service
come out to clean up and replace the linens.*

Ria

"Oh, my. Look at that!" Lena stopped the vehicle as Glen Eyrie Castle came into view. The stone carriage house to the left and a smaller pinkish stone building to the right were dwarfed by the massive red stone Tudor castle. Surrounded by pines and accented with the brilliant white background of recently fallen snow, the castle stood in stark contrast to the pine-dotted, snow-laden hill behind it. Lena thought the scene looked like something straight out of a fairy tale.

Lena parked the car, and the two women made their way over a small bridge and up the stone steps to the front entrance of Glen Eyrie castle. Two large, iron-studded wooden doors arched and came to a subtle point at the top. They were framed perfectly by masonry architrave, and large iron carriage lights adorned either side of the doors.

From the drawstring pouch Ria had given her, Lena removed the antique barrel skeleton key and inserted it into the keyhole of the door on the right side. The key turned easily, and the core made a sound similar to fingernails on a chalkboard, followed by a solid *kerplunk* as the iron bolt settled into the unlocked position. She removed the key, turned the iron knob, opened the heavy door, and stepped inside. Jasmyn followed, closing the door behind her.

The darkness of the interior of the castle foyer was a stark contrast to the bright afternoon sun reflected by the snow. Lena heard Jasmyn catch her breath as her eyes adjusted to the dim interior of the foyer. Perfectly polished wood paneled walls gleamed softly in the yellow light cast by two iron wall sconces. Two pocket doors were barely visible in the wall to the left.

Next to the pocket doors was an enormous fireplace with an ornately carved wood entablature above it that extended all the way to the ceiling which, by Lena's estimation, was 15 feet high. The jambs on either side of the fireplace were of matching, intricately carved wood next to red brick enclosures atop a grey slate hearth. Under the wood mantle was a curved metal fireplace hood with three embossed fleurs-de-lis in the middle of the hood, crisscross brass decorative strips and nail head trim. Three large brass round plates and a kerosene lamp with a curved metal handle sat on the mantle.

To the left of the fireplace was the suit of armor Ria had mentioned in her note. At least six feet tall and wearing a red velvet skirt with short gold fringe trim, the dull metal knight offered an imposing first impression. Neatly stacked wood was arranged to the right of the fireplace, and an old copper bucket held pinecones, lengthy dried grasses, and a box of 12-inch matches.

A large archway to the right of the fireplace and a grandiose curved wood staircase to the right of the archway beckoned the women to explore the remainder of the castle. Lena and Jasmyn left their belongings in the foyer and for more than an hour explored the castle. Jasmyn carried a notepad and took notes at Lena's request. The castle boasted 67 rooms including 17 bedrooms, each immaculately furnished with antique furniture and fine art from around the world.

The great hall on the second floor was more than 3,000 square feet. It was lit by massive chandeliers that hung from a 30-foot arched wood ceiling; it also featured an impressive stone fireplace and what appeared to be a choir or observation balcony. A second hall appeared to be a grand dining room, though a smaller dining room and library closer to the kitchen on the first floor offered a more intimate eating space option. The castle also boasted a music room, a sunroom, several sitting rooms, and 24 fireplaces. Each room, including the 12 bathrooms, was equipped with a lighter next to either a hurricane lantern, candle, or kerosene lantern.

Lena and Jasmyn marveled at how the castle had been decorated and preserved. From original windows and detailed ceilings to antique hardware on doors and cabinets, the castle was masterfully maintained. Every room and piece of furniture in Glen Eyrie castle, with exception of the modernized industrial kitchen and a small elevator from the reception hall to the second floor, felt authentic to the late 1800s. Lena believed the appraisal might come in as high as $42 million.

Lena chose a bedroom for the weekend that had immaculate wood trim around the doors and windows, a king bed, two lounge chairs and a writing desk. It had a glass atrium with a patio set, a cushioned window seat and unique stained-glass windows. Jasmyn selected a room across the hall from the room Lena had chosen that was decorated entirely in cornflower blue. It had a large velvet lounge chair, an intricately carved antique writing desk, and stunning views of the nearby red rock canyon.

Curious about the contents of the wine cellar, Jasmyn and Lena decided to explore the cellar. They headed down the artfully carved wooden staircase from the second floor to the main floor. Through the large window on the intermediate landing between the second floor and main floor where the stairs changed direction, they noticed Kacie and Gwyn ascending the stone stairs to the castle entrance. They headed to the foyer to greet Gwyn and Kacie.

"Lawd have mercy!" exclaimed Kacie in her thick Kentucky drawl as she entered the main door. "I always did want me a knight in shining armor, and I love that this particular sexy iron knight is holding a lovely flower!"

Looking in the direction of the suit of armor, Lena was stunned to see a bright red flower in the knight's right hand. She was certain the flower had not been there when she and Jasmyn arrived, and it occurred to her that the bloom was similar to the spiky red flowers in a dream she'd had two nights before about walking through an aspen grove.

She looked at Jasmyn for confirmation that the flower had not been in the knight's armored hand before. The intern's mouth hung open slightly, eyes wide as she met Lena's gaze. Lena shrugged her shoulders, assuming she had simply failed to notice the flower when they arrived.

While Gwyn and Kacie explored the castle and chose their rooms, Jasmyn helped Lena put the groceries away in the kitchen. Neither spoke for several minutes. Finally, Jasmyn asked if Lena had noticed the red flower in the knight's hand when they had first entered the castle. Lena, avoiding eye contact, shook her head.

Convinced that the flower might be a sign of paranormal activity in the castle, Jasmyn articulated plans to set up a camera to record the suit of armor overnight. Lena nodded quietly and, using the gift of bourbon from Jasmyn's father, made four apricot bourbon and ginger cocktails. She placed the drinks on a handled tray, which she handed to Jasmyn and sent her to start a fire in the main reception hall fireplace.

A brilliant orange glow from the setting sun outside the kitchen window was a welcome distraction for Lena as she prepared a plate of almonds, dark chocolate, and dried apricots. She shivered, noticing that the kitchen seemed at least five degrees colder than the rest of the castle. Lena picked up the plate of hors d'oeuvres and carried it to the main reception hall adjacent to the foyer where Gwyn, Kacie and Jasmyn were already settled in leather wingback chairs near the fireplace.

"Really nice snack and beverage combo, Lena. I have taught you well!" Gwyn winked at her older sister. "Thanks for the invitation – this place is phenomenal! Being here feels like stepping back in time – ought we to be wearing corsets, ladies?"

Raising her glass, Lena responded. "Here's to a corset-free weekend with good company, good food, good wine, and good memories." By the warmth of the fire, she filled the women in on the history of the castle, the ghostly claims made by Ria, David, and Ben, and her potential opportunity to sell the property. While Lena prepared a second round of drinks, Jasmyn read Ria's welcome note aloud.

"Interesting stuff, but I don't believe in ghosts" Gwyn proclaimed. "It could be spooky and fun to tour the place at night, though!"

"Agreed," said Kacie. "I'll believe that sort of malarkey if I see it. There is no such thing as ghosts."

Without warning two loud, long screeching sounds like metal scraping against metal emanated from the adjacent foyer. The women exchanged brief nervous glances as Lena and Kacie sprang from their chairs. Seconds later the unexpected crash of two metal objects colliding in the foyer elicited a brief, high-pitched shriek from Jasmyn.

With a feisty, determined expression on her freckled face, Kacie took the glass from Lena's hand and placed it on the side table. She grabbed Lena's elbow and cautiously tugged her toward the foyer. Gwyn placed an arm around Jasmyn's shoulder. Huddled together they followed Kacie and Lena who, as they cautiously rounded the corner to the foyer, stopped abruptly.

"What in tarnation… that's cotton pickin' impossible!" Kacie exclaimed breathlessly as the color drained from her face.

The suit of armor, which had previously stood to the left of the fireplace facing the large entry door, now stood squarely in front of the fireplace facing the main floor reception hall from which the women had just emerged. The visor portion of the helmet that covered the mouth and nose, which had been closed before, was now open. Lena had the uneasy feeling that there was something inside the suit, and that it was staring at them.

"Dios nos proteja del mal," Jasmyn muttered.

"English, Jasmyn" Lena snapped as she fumbled for her cell phone so she could call the security guard at the guard shack.

With a shaky voice Jasmyn replied, "Sorry. It means God protect us from evil."

Chapter Two Recipes

Chicken & Dumplings

    4 raw chicken breasts, diced into ½" cubes

    1 stick salted butter

    1 clove minced garlic

    2 T Penzey's ® Herbes de Provence

    1 bay leaf

    1 t. pepper

    1 1/2 t. salt

    Dash of cayenne pepper

    12 c. water

    1 can Pillsbury Grands ® biscuits

Melt butter over medium heat. Add garlic and cubed chicken; sauté until chicken is cooked through. Add all remaining ingredients except biscuits and bring to a boil.

While soup is simmering, make dumplings from biscuits as follows: Roll biscuits on a floured surface to ¼" thick. Slice each rolled biscuit into 1" squares, and drop individually into simmering soup, stirring occasionally.

Simmer 15-20 minutes or until dumplings are shrunken and firm.

Apricot Bourbon & Ginger Cocktails

¼ c. Blanton's bourbon

1/3 c. ginger ale

1 T. apricot schnapps

1 lime wedge

3 bourbon-soaked cherries

Pour bourbon, ginger ale, and apricot schnapps over ice in a glass. Squeeze lime wedge into glass, stir gently, and garnish with cherries either in the bottom of the glass or on a toothpick.

— CHAPTER 3 —

An Officer and a Gentleman

The security guard on duty checked the castle thoroughly for signs of an intruder while the women waited in the foyer, keeping a watchful eye on the iron knight. The guard returned having found no sign of an intruder. After assuring the visitors that they were alone in the castle, the guard moved the suit of armor back to its original position. Sensing the women's trepidation, he smiled reassuringly.

"Ladies, truth is strange things happen here at Glen Eyrie, but no one has been hurt as far as I know," he said. "I see three spirits from time to time outside. There is a man in an old-fashioned brown pinstriped wool suit, a dark-haired White lady in a long blue dress, and a Black lady in an old-fashioned maid uniform. Seems to me they just want folks to know they are here." The guard tipped his hat and left, closing the large wood door behind him.

Gwyn locked the door behind the guard, exhaled sharply, and turned to face the other women. Jasmyn was slouched, leaning into Kacie's protective embrace while chewing nervously on her fingernails. Lena was seated on the hearth staring nervously at the red spiky flower in the iron knight's hand.

Gwyn cleared her throat, and then spoke in a confident, authoritative tone. "I don't know what to think about this, Lena, but I do know it is time to get dinner started. The salmon has been marinating all day. How about someone help me in the kitchen while the other two set the table and find a good bottle of red wine in the cellar? We will need something full-bodied and fruity. Dinner will be ready in about 45 minutes."

"I'll help you, Gwyn" Jasmyn offered quickly. "I sure as hell am not going to the cellar right now – if I were a ghost that is where I would hang out. Besides, I don't want to be alone."

Great. Isn't the cellar where bad things happen in horror movies? Lena brushed the thought aside. Mindful of Ria's caution about lighting, she took a lighter and kerosene lamp off the hearth in the foyer and followed Kacie toward the cellar. Outside the cellar door Lena and Kacie paused to discuss what had occurred, though neither could offer a rational explanation for the movement of the iron knight.

The stairs to the cellar seemed creepier to Lena than they had earlier in the afternoon, so she was grateful for Kacie's courage and eagerness to descend first. For a White, privileged southern belle Kacie had the bravado and vocabulary of a sailor – something Lena had long admired. Kacie flipped the light switch on. Dim sconces cast a subtle yellow light revealing grey stone stairs. At the bottom of the stairs Lena could see grey stone floors and walls.

Kacie and Lena descended the stone stairs cautiously. The stone cellar ceiling was supported by large wood beams Old furniture covered with white sheets and a few neatly stacked boxes lined the cellar walls. Hoping the arched wooden door nearest to them would lead to the wine room, Lena pressed the latch and pushed the door open. The door groaned loudly as Lena pushed it open, causing her to burst out laughing.

"Castles, ghosts, and creaking doors, oh my!" Kacie said between giggles from behind Lena, skipping like Dorothy from the Wizard of Oz. "Of course, the cellar door to the wine room in a creepy old castle creaks! Of course it does!"

The wine room held several hundred bottles of wine. A large electric cooler for white wines took up most of the back wall. Countless bottles of red wine were nestled into stone insets along the left and right sides of the room. The insets were labeled with horizontal engraved metal plaques affixed to the stone under each inset. Lena selected a bottle of Rosso di Montalcino for dinner, pleasantly surprised to find such a new wine in the old cellar.

Lena and Kacie laughed again at the creaking of the wine room door as they exited and closed the door behind them. As they ascended the cellar stairs Lena could not help but feel somewhat foolish for having lugged the lighter and kerosene lantern down to the cellar. After ascending the cellar stairs Lena went to return the lamp and lighter to the foyer while Kacie took the wine to the dining room. As she entered the foyer Lena was privately relieved to see the suit of armor exactly where the security guard had left it, though she also noticed that the red flower the knight had held in its hand earlier was gone. She headed to the dining room to join the other women and enjoy the dinner that Gwyn had prepared.

Kacie, Jasmyn, and Gwyn were already seated at the long dining table, the end of which had been elegantly set for four, when Lena arrived at the doorway to the dining room. She smiled, eager to enjoy their company, but her smile quickly faded. Just as Lena crossed the threshold to the dining room the heavy, velvet-trimmed chair at her place setting inexplicably pulled away from the table, then angled its seat toward her. It was as if a gentleman had pulled the chair out for her, but no one was touching the chair. Eyes wide and mouth agape, Lena looked at the other women as if to verify what she had seen, but they were all staring in silence at the now motionless chair.

After several seconds, Kacie muttered "bourbon." She sprang from her seat and departed the room. Gwyn glanced from the chair to Lena, then back to the chair. Although Lena's instinct was to turn and run, she found herself somehow compelled to walk toward the chair.

Lena slowly and cautiously approached the chair, vaguely aware of Kacie re-entering the room and the stares of Gwyn and Jasmyn. Stopping in front of the chair she nodded slightly to someone who she could not see and said, "Thank you." Her heart pounding so loudly she could hear it, Lena sat in the chair and waited briefly in case whatever force had moved the chair decided to push it in for her. Sensing no movement, she scooted the chair in and placed her napkin in her lap.

Still standing just inside the doorway between the kitchen and dining room with the bottle of bourbon in one hand, Kacie muttered "glasses," and disappeared back into the kitchen. She re-emerged momentarily with a serving tray, on which her shaking hands carried the remaining bourbon and five glasses. Quietly she poured a glass of bourbon and served one to each of the women. After pouring the fifth glass, which she placed on the table in front of the chair next to Lena, she quietly returned to her own seat.

"Who… who is that one for?" Jasmyn asked with a quiet, shaky voice.

"General Panton." Kacie said, her eyes cast downward.

Gwyn interrupted several seconds of uncomfortable silence by clearing her throat softly. She raised her glass and nodded to the other women, who glanced at each other nervously but also raised their glasses. "I would like to propose a toast to General Panton, who has established himself as both an officer and a gentleman."

"Here, here" Lena replied breathlessly, concerned that her heart was still beating terribly hard. She stared at the glass that had been set out for General Panton, hoping desperately that it would not move.

"To the General. *Bourbon te hace valiente*" Jasmyn replied politely. The other women looked at her with some annoyance, wondering what she had just said in Spanish. "It means bourbon makes you brave."

"God, I hope you're right, Jasmyn. Bottoms up y'all," Kacie said before gulping down her entire drink. She poured herself another bit of bourbon and passed the bottle to Gwyn.

Lena recalled studying group hallucinations in a social psychology class as an undergraduate student, but she felt certain that she and the others had actually witnessed the chair move seemingly on its own. The four women sat in silence as they sipped their second servings of straight bourbon, glancing occasionally at the glass of bourbon Kacie had set out for General Panton. After several minutes of tense silence, Jasmyn politely suggested that she help Gwyn set the food out on the buffet table for dinner, and the pair headed to the kitchen.

Emboldened by the bourbon, Kacie moved a silver tray and matching candle sticks from the middle of the buffet table to the far end of the dining table and walked to the window, where she paused to gaze at the night sky. She confided in Lena that she thought the house might really be haunted. Lena joined her friend at the window and concurred that a rational explanation for the knight's movement and the chair situation was difficult to conceive.

The lights flickered slightly, prompting Kacie to remove a hurricane lamp from the fireplace, light it, and place it on the dining table.

"Just in case the lights go out," Kacie said softly. Lena nodded and finished her bourbon, wrinkling her nose as the liquor warmed her throat. Jasmyn was right about bourbon making you feel brave, she thought to herself. Lena did feel a little bit braver, though she did not particularly appreciate straight liquor of any kind. Kacie scoffed at her friend's sour facial expression and poured glasses of wine while Gwyn and Jasmyn set the food out on the buffet table.

"OK, ladies… dinner is served. Come get your plates." Feeling the effects of the bourbon, Gwyn offered a curtsey and gestured toward the buffet table. "This evening I have prepared for you fine ladies a tart cherry balsamic glazed salmon, lemon risotto with mushrooms and asparagus, and a spinach salad with mandarin oranges and dried cherries tossed gently in a balsamic reduction." The women filled their plates and enjoyed an uneventful return to their respective seats at the end of the long dining table.

"I must say, Gwyn, I do love having a chef as a sister! Culinary school was absolutely one of the best investments I ever made. This salmon is to die for!" Lena closed her eyes and savored her second bite. Kacie agreed, and Jasmyn suggested that the Panton family had most likely enjoyed similarly fine meals every night.

"Thank you. I appreciate having a sister who has obscenely rich real estate clients. You do invite me to some amazing places." Gwyn sipped thoughtfully on her wine. "You know, I could do without the weird happenings, but this castle is the most beautiful place I have ever seen. In the morning I want to explore the rest of the property. Hopefully, there are a couple of hiking trails outside."

The women's dinner conversation centered around plans to explore the carriage house, the smaller pink building that had once served as a schoolhouse used for the Panton children, and the wooded acreage of the estate the following day. After helping herself to the glass of bourbon Kacie had poured for General Panton, Jasmyn shifted the conversation by sharing her plan to set up the borrowed night vision camera for the evening. She wanted to aim the camera at the iron knight in the foyer. Kacie hesitantly confessed that she preferred to not sleep alone; Jasmyn felt the same way, so the two decided to share the room Jasmyn had chosen earlier in the day.

Kacie and Jasmyn went upstairs to move Kacie's suitcase to Jasmyn's room while Gwyn and Lena cleared the table after dinner. As the two sisters rinsed dishes and loaded the commercial grade dishwasher Gwyn shared an appreciation for the large kitchen, which had been recently updated with the finest culinary equipment. Lena concurred, but noted that the modern kitchen contrasted peculiarly with the décor and feel of other rooms in the castle.

Just then a chilling scream followed by thunderous laughter and the dull dragging sound of chairs being moved around on wood floors emanated from the dining room as Kacie and Jasmyn pushed the chairs back up to the dining table. Gwyn and Lena entered, amused to see the two women laughing so hard that each were wiping away tears. Following a rather unfeminine, laughter-induced snort, Kacie explained between short, breathless giggles that Jasmyn had been spooked by movement she had seen in the large mirror above the buffet table, only to realize that it was her own reflection.

Following a hearty laugh at Jasmyn's expense, the four women decided that a nighttime room-by-room tour of the castle was in order once the video camera was set up in the foyer. Gwyn and Jasmyn left to retrieve the recording equipment Jasmyn had borrowed, and everyone agreed to meet in the foyer.

Lena gathered the cloth napkins and tossed them down the laundry chute she had noticed in the kitchen while Kacie carefully returned the silver serving tray and matching candlesticks to their original places on the buffet table in the dining room. Kacie extinguished the hurricane lamp on the dining table as Lena re-entered the dining room.

"What do you suppose this place is worth?" Kacie asked.

Lena did some quick calculations in her mind, then responded. "Probably in the neighborhood of 40 to 45 million. The castle is incredible, and the views are gorgeous. The recent population growth in Colorado Springs makes the location desirable. If the place really is haunted, though, that could be a factor. It is too bad, really. But the castle belongs to Ria now, and she is determined to sell it."

Without warning the lights in the dining room went out and a female voice harshly whispered *"Nooooo!"*. Kacie grabbed Lena's hand tightly as the room plunged into darkness and Lena sucked in a sharp breath. *Swoosh.* The sound of something - a skirt, perhaps – was followed quickly by footsteps exiting the room rapidly.

The footsteps were light, and the *click clack* of each step sounded as if they might belong to a woman wearing heeled shoes. Frozen with fear, Lena and Kacie clung to each other in the dark dining room as they listened to the footsteps run past the reception room fireplace, through the foyer, up the grand staircase, and gradually fade as they progressed down the long second floor hallway.

When the footsteps were no longer audible the dining room lights abruptly turned back on and an eerie silence filled the room. Lena took a deep breath and exhaled it slowly as she attempted to regain her composure. Arms linked, she and Kacie crept cautiously out of the dining room and through the reception hall; both were relieved to see Jasmyn and Gwyn huddled together, descending the grand staircase.

Whispering as if someone – or something – might overhear their conversation, they exchanged experiences. Jasmyn and Gwyn had also heard the footsteps and had been temporarily frozen in place on the staircase landing when they experienced a strong, frigid breeze rush past them.

"Apparently the ghost doesn't want Ria to sell the place," Jasmyn remarked sarcastically, clutching the borrowed night-vision video camera firmly to her chest. With trepidation she departed the huddled group in the reception hall and crossed the threshold into the foyer. Gwyn followed and, after scrutinizing the knight to ensure it had not moved, began setting up the tripod.

While she set up the camera, Jasmyn proposed a plan for exploring the castle together. "If we don't turn on any lights, then the ghosts – or whatever – can't scare us by turning them off. I say we stay together and explore in the dark. We can use the flashlight function on our cell phones to light the way.

But one thing is certain – we should stay together." Jasmyn noticed Lena's right eyebrow raise dramatically.

Mindful of Ria's warning that cell phone and flashlight batteries were frequently drained in the castle, Lena suggested they carry lanterns with them. Kacie asserted that hurricane lanterns would be too heavy to carry around and if accidentally dropped, the kerosene could start a fire. It was Gwyn who had a solution: she had noticed an old metal and glass enclosed candle lantern with a handle in the kitchen window and suggested they could take turns carrying it.

Jasmyn set the camera to record and together the women returned to the kitchen, turning out the lights along the way. Gwyn lit the candle in the lantern and slipped the lighter into the pocket of her oversized plaid flannel shirt. Kacie turned on the LED flashlight she had brought for the weekend, and Lena turned on her cell phone flashlight.

Cell phone in hand, Kacie reached toward the light switch near the door leading from the kitchen to the dining room. Looking seriously at the others, she said "We are intelligent, brave women. Obviously, ghosts can scare us, but I do not believe they can hurt us. I am wondering if maybe they just have a story that needs to be told. Let's explore and enjoy the experience. Everybody ready?" The women nodded and Kacie took a deep breath before turning out the kitchen light.

For two and a half hours they explored the castle's 67 rooms. Their cell phones were all dead within the first hour, so the candle lantern and Kacie's flashlight were the only sources of light for most of the evening. Though the castle seemed oddly quiet, nothing out of the ordinary happened and the women enjoyed the spooky, dimly lit experience.

That night Lena dreamt again of the aspen grove with green shrubs that bore red flowers. This time the dream was more vivid; the smell of pine and the warmth of the sun were tangible, and a man stood beside her. Her right hand pressed against her belly, and tears, slightly chilled by a light breeze, ran down her face. Looking down at her trembling right hand, Lena realized she was wearing a full, long black skirt with a white ruffled apron.

"No one must know," the man's voice said. "But I will take care of both of you. I promise." The man placed a gentle hand under her chin and tilted her face upwards, forcing her to look at him. Lena looked up at the man, and into the eyes of General Wynston Jamison Panton.

Chapter Three Recipes

Tart Cherry Balsamic Glazed Salmon

6 5-oz. salmon filets

1 T. butter

3 cloves garlic, minced

2 T. white wine

1 ¼ c. balsamic vinegar (for reduction)

1/4 c. tart cherry juice concentrate

1 T. Dijon mustard

1 T. oregano

1 T. honey

Salt and pepper to taste

Directions:

1. In small saucepan, bring balsamic vinegar to a boil. Reduce temperature and simmer 10 – 15 minutes until it is reduced by half. Pour reduction into a bowl to cool.

2. Melt butter in a clean saucepan over medium heat. Add garlic and sauté until soft (approximately 3 – 4 minutes).

3. Remove saucepan from heat. Add balsamic reduction and remaining ingredients to the sautéed garlic and whisk ingredients together well.

4. Place salmon filets in a large one-gallon zip-top plastic food storage bag. Pour whisked liquid over filets, seal bag, and place in refrigerator. Allow to marinate 4 – 6 hours.

5. Preheat oven to 400 degrees.

6. Place filets on a foil-lined baking sheet and drizzle with half of the marinade.

7. Bake uncovered for 10 to 14 minutes, or until flesh flakes easily with a fork.

8. Drizzle filets with remaining marinade; serve immediately.

— CHAPTER 4 —

The Woman in Blue

A chorus of loudly chirping birds outside her window woke Lena up earlier than she had hoped to rise on Saturday morning. Morning light peeked through the open curtains. Annoyed, Lena squeezed her eyes shut and rolled drowsily from her right side facing the windows over to her left side facing the antique writing desk. Gradually the noisy chattering of birds stopped completely. Grateful for the silence, Lena began to drift back to sleep.

Scritch scratch. Scritch scratch. Scritch scratch. A faint scratching sound seemed to come from directly in front of her. *Scritch scratch. Scritch scratch.* Feeling a sudden chill, Lena burrowed deeper into the blankets.

Scritch scratch. Scritch scratch. Surrendering to the persistent scratching sound, Lena opened her eyes slightly. Seated at the writing desk was a woman in a long blue silk dress with puffy shoulders and fitted sleeves. Uncertain whether she was asleep or awake, Lena rubbed her eyes and blinked, realizing with clarity that she was indeed awake. The woman at the desk turned her head slightly to the left and looked at Lena, who suddenly found herself unable to move or breathe.

The woman's brown hair was piled neatly on top of her head with a few curls trailing softly across the squared jaw of her porcelain face. She was attractive, slightly plump and appeared to be in her late forties. The expression on the woman's face was one of concern. Her posture was straight, and she held an old-fashioned black fountain pen in her right hand.

Lena wanted to scream, but for some reason her body was frozen; she could only watch. The woman turned back to the desk, dipped the fountain pen in an ink well and wrote quickly for several seconds. *Scritch scratch. Scritch scratch. Scritch scratch.* Then, setting her pen down softly, the woman rose delicately from the chair. Lena could hear the woman's long blue skirt shift in the eerie silence. Slowly the woman turned and faced Lena, smiling slightly. As their eyes met Lena knew that the woman looked familiar to her and Lena realized with horror that, despite the woman's completely solid form, she was from another time.

"You must claim what is yours. It is only right, Selena" the woman said softly. The woman had a British accent and, though she wore a faint smile on her face, Lena sensed a great sadness in the woman. The woman's deep-set brown eyes remained locked with Lena's. Gradually becoming less solid, the woman raised her right arm and pointed at the writing desk. Lena shifted her gaze to the desk briefly, then looked back toward the woman in the blue dress, but the woman had vanished.

Startled by the sound of light, feminine heeled footsteps receding quickly down the hall, Lena realized she had been holding her breath. She took two large gasps of air before regaining control of her body and releasing a terrified scream. She sat upright and gasped for air, grateful for the pitter patter sound of running bare feet as Kacie, Gwen, and Jasmyn approached her room. Gwyn burst through the door and leapt into the bed, wrapping her arms protectively around her older sister. Kacie and Jasmyn followed closely behind Gwyn.

Violent trembles rocked Lena's body and tears streamed down her face. She struggled for breath and grasped Gwyn's arms tightly. Intellectually Lena knew she was hyperventilating but she was helpless to stop it. She felt her eyes begin to roll back in her head. Kacie crawled across the bed and quickly straddled Lena's legs. She took Lena's face firmly in her hands, forcing Lena to look at her.

"Lena, darlin', I need you to try to breathe in through your nose and then out through your mouth slowly like me," Kacie said seriously. It took several minutes of coached breathing, but slowly Lena's breathing normalized, and Kacie released her hold on Lena's face.

"A gh... gh... gh! A gh... gh..." Lena tried desperately to speak but was still too panicked to form words.

"Shhh, Lena, don't try to talk quite yet. Just breathe, okay?" Gwyn spoke soothingly and continued to hold Lena tightly, as Jasmyn and Kacie watched with concern. Eventually collapsing into deep sobs, Lena buried her face into Gwyn's shoulder. Gradually she began to calm, raising her face only briefly to accept a box of tissues from Jasmyn.

"Th... thanks," Lena stammered. "A gh... ghost was in here, guys. I ss... saw a woman at the desk writing." The women exchanged glances as Lena, still trembling violently drew in a long, ragged breath and exhaled it slowly. Jasmyn got off the bed and strode to the writing desk. She picked up a piece of tan wood pulp paper with uneven edges that had intricate handwriting on it.

"Madre María de Dios," she said, eyes wide as she handed the paper to Kacie. Jasmyn made the sign of the cross by using her right hand to touch her forehead, the middle of her chest, left shoulder, and right shoulder.

Struggling at times to decipher the delicate Spencerian cursive, Kacie read the letter aloud.

My heart became too fragile for altitude thus I dwelt on the east coast and in England mostly. The housemaid, Mitilde, lived in the garret and worked for wages and schooling expenses. Wynston returned to our Colorado castle after my heart succumbed and Mitilde was a comfort to my beloved. Alas, amorous congress is inevitable when a man is lonely. Hasten to find the letters in the dressing table. The truth is your lineage.

M.

After an awkward silence Jasmyn asked, "Was this letter here when we arrived yesterday, Lena? What is a garret, and who is 'M'?"

"Yeah, and what in the world is amorous congress?" Kacie asked, clearly perplexed.

"Lena, I believe you that you saw something." Gwyn chimed in calmly. "You are the coolest cucumber I know, and you are obviously rattled to your core. I might even believe that this note was written by someone or something otherworldly. But there is nothing here now, and I need time to process." Gwyn suggested that she get the eggs benedict casserole started, and that Lena could share exactly what happened with the others over breakfast after she had time to collect her thoughts.

Kacie offered to stay in the room while Lena got ready, to which Lena nodded gratefully. Gwyn left to start breakfast and Kacie returned to her room to grab a change of clothes so she could get ready in Lena's room. Still shaking, Lena remained in the bed with the blankets clutched to her chin. Jasmyn gently pulled back the blankets and offered a hand to help Lena up, but she recoiled and sucked in a sharp gasp at the sight of Lena's feet, which were caked in dried mud and blood.

"Kacie, come quick," Jasmyn shouted. "Lena's feet are bleeding – something is very wrong!"

A nurse for more than 15 years, Kacie never traveled without a first aid kit. "Lena, what happened to your feet? Did you sleepwalk outside or something?" Kacie knelt in front of her oldest and dearest friend, who offered no response but sat motionless, expressionless on the bed. Concerned, Kacie started the shower and helped Lena to the bathroom.

The warm water hurt Lena's feet, so she showered quickly. She wrapped herself in a towel and sat on the side of the bed. Horrified and frightened, Lena was still unable to speak. What had happened to her feet? Lena could not fathom any possible answer. Everything had been just fine when she went to sleep the prior evening. Kacie rubbed antibiotic cream over the raw patches and deep cuts on the bottom of Lena's feet, then wrapped them with gauze. She loaned Lena a pair of white cotton socks, then helped Lena to the chair at the writing desk, stripped the soiled sheets from the bed, and went to the bathroom to take a quick shower.

When Kacie emerged from the bathroom, she was surprised to see Lena still seated at the writing desk, staring out the window with a blank expression. "Okay, my friend. The worst thing that could happen would be for you to fall down the slippery wood stairs in those socks, so let's navigate them together." She held out a hand, which Lena accepted. Arms linked, the two slowly made their way down the stairs. They paused briefly at the foyer to steal a glance at the knight, which remained in its proper location.

Several inches of snow had fallen overnight, and the dining room was chilly, so Jasmyn lit a fire in the dining room fireplace to warm the room. While the others ate breakfast and sipped mimosas, Lena told them everything about the strange fireplace incident at her condo, the two dreams about walking in an aspen grove, and every detail about the woman in blue. When she finished the room fell silent for several minutes, except for the occasional popping sound from the dining room fireplace.

Finally, Jasmyn cleared her throat and spoke. "I did some research while Gwyn was cooking. A garret is an old-fashioned word for attic," she said softly, removing the cloth napkin from her lap and placing it on the table before continuing. "And get this – back in the day, 'amorous congress' was a polite term used to refer to having sex." The other three women stared at Jasmyn as if waiting for more. "The signature 'M' could have been short for Marie. That was the name of General Panton's wife, though it is well documented that he preferred to call her 'Queenie.'"

Gwyn took a deep breath and looked at her sister as if requesting permission, but Lena had finally decided to eat and was loading a helping of eggs benedict casserole onto her plate. "I can add something interesting," Gwyn offered cautiously. "The letter referred to a maid named Mitilde. Our grandmother's name was Mitilde, and her name was spelled the same way as presented in the letter. We called her 'Granny M'. I looked her information up on the internet while I was waiting for the casserole to be done – our Granny M was born in 1922 and passed away in 2001."

Jasmyn placed her cell phone on the table, tapping at it furiously. "Queenie died in 1894, and the General died in 1909. Your granny was born years after the general passed. Besides, isn't your family from Georgia?"

"Yes." Lena replied, casting a cautious glance at Gwyn. "Our great-grandmother on our mother's side was a twin – they were half Black. We do not know much about her parents, but I remember mom telling me that the mother had been out west working for a White family, and when she returned to Georgia, she was pregnant and married to a White man. But it would be pretty far-fetched to think they were in any way connected to General Panton."

"Weird" Kacie said. "Forgive me if you find this offensive, but neither of you look like you have black ancestors. I have known you for years, Lena. Why haven't you mentioned this before?"

Gwyn furrowed her brow. "Well, Kacie, looks can be deceiving. Lena, this could explain how great-grandma Willi came to own a house and a small peanut farm. If you think about it, owning property would have been pretty unusual for a mixed-race family at that time in American history, especially in Georgia."

Lena raised a skeptical right eyebrow at her sister. "Don't be silly, Gwyn. Kacie, I guess I never mentioned it because it never seemed important." Lena picked up her phone to send a text to Ria.

Hi, Ria. Well, you were right – this place is haunted. Are you familiar with a room called a garret? I think that is an old term for 'attic'. If so, where would access to such a room be located? Lena

Not an attic per se, but there is an old maid's quarters. In the 2nd floor hallway past the first few bedrooms, you'll see an alcove to the left. The small door that starts about halfway to the ceiling is the entrance – there's a built-in ladder to it on the wall. I went in once, and it's nothing special. There's another similar one behind the General's smoking room – look for the brass ring on the wall to the left of the fireplace. Enjoy exploring!

OK – thanks! BTW, I saw a woman with brown hair in a blue dress in my room this morning. Is that Queenie?

I suspect so. BTW, I dreamed about you last night. You were walking barefoot at night in the woods, and it was snowing. Crazy, right?

Yeah – crazy.

Jasmyn and Gwen decided they would go in search of the garrets after breakfast while Kacie and Lena searched the grounds to see if an aspen grove like the one in Lena's dreams existed on the property. Gwyn convinced Kacie and Jasmyn to clean up the breakfast dishes so she and Lena could have a few moments alone.

In Lena's room Gwyn pulled Lena out into the glass atrium and called their uncle, Billy, on speaker phone. He did not answer, so Gwyn left a message. "Hi Uncle Billy – it's Gwyn. I am in Colorado Springs with Lena for a long weekend. Hey, we are in need of some information about our family history. What do you know about Granny M's parents and grandparents?

Here is what I need to know. Granny M's mother was Willi, right? Willi was half Black. Who was her father, and what do you know about her mother? How did great-grandma Willi's parents come to own the peanut farm? This is pretty important, Uncle Billy. Can you call me or Lena as soon as you get this message? Or better yet, maybe you could e-mail details if you have them. Thanks, Uncle Billy. Love you!"

Lena called Ria and told her about her feet. Ria was stunned because of the similarity of Lena's situation to the dream she'd had the previous night about Lena walking barefoot in the snowy woods. Ria suggested that Lena use the three-wheeled all-terrain vehicle from the storage barn behind the carriage house to explore the property. Lena had driven similar ATVs before while visiting David's ranch, and the truth was that her feet were too tender for hiking. She thanked Ria for allowing her to borrow the ATV and promised to wear a helmet.

Kacie and Lena met in the foyer and donned coats, scarves, and gloves. Kacie excitedly flung open the front door revealing the vast castle grounds, which were beautifully blanketed by an inch of fresh snow that had fallen the previous night. Lena was about to wonder aloud which direction they should head once they were on the ATV, but she never asked the question. Instead, both women stood just inside the castle threshold, shocked to see footprints in the snow leading away from the entrance, and a set of muddy footprints leading back to the entrance. Lena could only assume the footprints were her own.

"Well butter me up and call me a biscuit, Lena. I guess you really did sleepwalk last night. You are lucky you didn't freeze to death!" Kacie looked at her friend with concern. Lena blinked back tears, shaking her head, and staring with disbelief at the footprints. Kacie took Lena's gloved hand in her own, and the two friends walked in silence to the carriage house.

They entered the carriage house using the security code Ria had provided and found the key ring, which they used to unlock the door to the steepled storage barn behind the cottage. After donning helmets, the two set out on a red all-terrain vehicle to explore the wooded property of the Glen Eyrie estate. Lena drove, and Kacie rode behind her.

Lena maneuvered the ATV slowly, following the footprints in the snow and enjoying the pristine castle grounds. Snow-laden pines and bare aspen offered a contrast to the jagged, snow-capped red sedimentary rocks that seemed to jut from the earth. She brought the vehicle to a slow stop when a movement in a clearing approximately 100 yards ahead caught her eye. She shushed Kacie and watched closely for a moment but did not see any more movement.

Hoping that the movement had been caused by a deer rather than a bear or mountain lion, Lena drove the ATV cautiously through an aspen grove among short green shrubs to the clearing, where the footprints in the snow abruptly stopped. Lena turned off the ATV as Kacie let go of her waist and jumped off the vehicle. Lena remained on the ATV sitting in dumbfounded silence. The aspen grove and short green shrubs were nearly identical to the clearing she had dreamt of twice, and the smell of pine that she remembered from her dream the night before hung in the chilly morning air.

Lena decided to share her realizations with Kacie, adding the only difference was that in both dreams the green bushes had red flowers on them. She looked closely at her friend, hoping that Kacie might find some piece of her bizarre story believable. Kacie walked to one of the round green bushes, kicked the snow off, and used her cell phone to take an up-close photo of the short shrub.

"There's an app on my phone called Picture Plant. You take a picture of a plant and the app tells you what kind of plant it..." Kacie's mouth dropped open. Making eye contact with Lena and pausing briefly, Kacie continued. "This is called an Indian paintbrush. It is native to the Rocky Mountain region and bears clusters of spiky red blooms in the spring."

Wide-eyed, Kacie walked to the ATV and handed Lena her phone so she could see a picture of the plant. "You're not going to believe this, Lena. The flower that was in the knight's hand last night was an Indian paintbrush, which is impossible because plants do not bloom in the middle of winter!"

Lena examined the picture and concurred with Kacie. "These are the flowers I saw in my dreams, Kacie, and you are correct," she said. "It is still winter – nothing is blooming yet. It would be impossible to find a bloom on any outside plant in Colorado right now."

Crack. The sharp sound of a snapping twig in the aspen grove to their left startled the two women, who instinctively grabbed each other's hands and looked toward the sound. In the shade of the aspens and pines stood a slightly transparent, attractive Black woman in her late twenties to early thirties. Her hair was pulled neatly away from her face, which bore a slight sad smile. The woman wore a long black dress with a full skirt, on top of which was layered a white ruffled Batiste apron. Her left arm was stretched out toward Kacie and Lena and in her left hand she held a spiky red flower, almost as if she were offering it to them.

Though the woman's mouth did not move, both Kacie and Lena clearly heard a woman's voice with a thick southern accent say, "They are my favorite." Then, as the woman quickly faded away, the same voice said, "Find the letters. Find the truth." Kacie and Lena stood huddled together staring at the aspen grove where the apparition had stood.

"Sweet Jesus" Kacie muttered. "You saw that, right?" Lena nodded, her gaze still fixed on the spot where the apparition of the maid had stood. "Did you hear her, too?" Again, Lena nodded. It was Kacie who moved first, walking cautiously toward the place where the woman had stood. Hand in hand the two friends inspected the snow for footprints but found nothing.

"Kacie, this is going to sound crazy, but I think I was her… I mean, in my dream last night!" Lena looked at her old friend with pleading eyes; she needed Kacie to believe her. "I remember looking down and noticing that I was wearing a long black skirt with a white apron that had a ruffled trim. We were here in this spot, me… I mean her… and General Panton. I felt unbearably sad and scared. I think they were saying goodbye."

Kacie frowned and looked at Lena with obvious concern. "Lena Thomas, are you telling me you think you are reincarnated and that you used to be that ghost lady?"

Shaking her head Lena replied, "No. But I think it is possible that she came to me in my dreams to tell me something, and that somehow she got me out here in the woods in the middle of the night. I don't want to believe I might have been possessed or something, but how else would you explain…." Lena looked down at her feet. Worried, Kacie shook her head and headed back towards the ATV.

The warmth of the late morning sun melted the heavy, wet spring snow as Lena and Kacie continued to explore the acres surrounding the castle for nearly two hours. They saw only majestic views, several elk, and some animal prints in the snow. Ready for lunch, they returned the ATV to the carriage house and headed back to the castle.

Once inside the foyer, Lena and Kacie removed their coats, boots, scarves, and gloves and laid them on the fireplace hearth to dry. Lena's feet hurt badly, so she walked gingerly to the adjacent main reception hall and settled into one of the large leather chairs with a footstool. Kacie went to the kitchen to get some ibuprofen for Lena and to check on the chicken tortilla soup Gwyn had started in the crock pot early that morning.

To accommodate Lena's need to elevate her feet, the women enjoyed lunch in the comfortable leather chairs by the fireplace in the main reception hall. Savoring the warm, spicy chicken tortilla soup, which Gwyn served with tortilla strips, shredded cheese, and sour cream, they shared with one another their experiences from the morning.

The garret in the second-floor hallway was locked, so Gwyn and Jasmyn had gone in search of the garret in the General's smoking room that Ria had mentioned in her text message. Unsure of which room that might be, they had gone room by room searching for one that had a brass ring on the wall to the left of the fireplace. They found what they were looking for in a wood-paneled room to the left of the foyer behind the wood pocket doors. Initially they had not noticed the door to the garret, but Jasmyn spied a small, tarnished brass ring pull in the wood paneling.

Upon entering the musty, windowless room Gwyn and Jasmyn had expected to find a small storage space. Instead, the room was larger than anticipated and contained an old bed neatly made with a handmade quilt. Next to the bed was a small table. There was also a dresser with a mirror and washbasin, a wardrobe closet, and an old black trunk which rested on the floor at the foot of the bed. Covered by cobwebs and dust, an old oil lantern on the side table seemed to be the only source of potential light in the dark room. The thickness of the dust and cobwebs led Gwyn to believe that no one had been in the room for many years.

In the wardrobe hung a high double-breasted black waistcoat and a low double-breasted black waistcoat with tails. Gwyn figured the room had likely been a butler's sleeping quarters. The dresser drawers contained only a folded blanket, and the trunk at the foot of the bed was locked. Jasmyn had attempted unsuccessfully to pick the trunk's lock with a bobby pin.

Jasmyn moved eagerly from a chair to the fireplace hearth. "I was on my hands and knees trying to pick the lock, and Gwyn was beside me shining the flashlight so I could see. Out of the blue the door to the room slammed shut and we heard heavy footsteps walking away through the smoking room and foyer!"

"Yeah, and you'll never believe what happened next!" Gwyn exclaimed. "At first the door wouldn't open! To be honest, it seemed like someone was pushing against it. After a few good shoves it opened right up but get this… that creepy iron knight was standing right in front of the door like it was watching what we were doing!"

Gwyn and Jasmyn explained that they had called the security guard at the gate who had searched the castle and moved the knight back to its proper location in the foyer. The security guard, who Jasmyn described as a 'gorgeous White guy named Dillon,' had jokingly referred to them as Thelma and Daphne and had asked when Shaggy and Scooby Doo would be arriving with more weed.

Dillon had told them that strange occurrences were just part of Glen Eyrie castle, and that he had been called to move the knight back to where it belonged several times in the three years he had worked as gate security. He told them that he had heard galloping horses run by the security gate a few times, but he never saw any horses. Dillon assured them that as far as he knew no one had ever been hurt by the spirits that were alleged to haunt the property, but he gave Jasmyn his personal cell phone number just in case anything else happened.

Chapter Four Recipes

Eggs Benedict Casserole

> 10 oz. chopped Canadian bacon
>
> 6 English muffins split, toasted, and cut into 1" pieces
>
> 8 eggs
>
> 2 c. milk
>
> ¼ t. ground mustard seed
>
> 1 t. onion powder
>
> ¼ t. paprika

OPTIONAL: Add a bag of frozen tater tots before adding the English muffins.

Directions:

1. The evening before serving, sprinkle half of the Canadian bacon in a greased 13"x9" baking dish; top with toasted English muffins chunks and the remaining Canadian bacon. In bowl, whisk together the eggs, milk, mustard seed, and onion powder; pour over the top and cover with plastic wrap. Refrigerate overnight.

2. In the morning, preheat the oven to 375 degrees.

3. Remove the plastic wrap and replace it with foil or an oven-proof lid. Bake for 35 minutes.

4. After 35 minutes, remove cover and bake for 10 – 15 more minutes until done (a knife inserted in the middle should come out clean).

While the casserole is in its final baking phase, make the Hollandaise sauce.

3 egg yolks

1 T. lemon juice

1/8 t. Cayenne pepper

1 stick (1/2 c.) salted butter.

<u>Directions:</u>

1. Place egg yolks, lemon juice, Cayenne pepper, and salt in a blender. Blend for 5-7 seconds on high.

2. After you remove the casserole from the oven sprinkle it with the paprika (it should sit for about 3 minutes before serving).

3. While the casserole rests, melt the butter in a covered microwavable dish until it is boiling hot.

4. With the blender running on medium speed, slowly drizzle the butter (which must be hot, not warm) into the mixture until it is emulsified.

5. Add cream if needed to thin.

Ladle Hollandaise sauce over servings of casserole and enjoy!

Crock Pot Chicken Tortilla Soup

1 pre-cooked rotisserie chicken

Two 15 oz. cans diced tomatoes with juice

10 oz. can red enchilada sauce

4 oz. can diced green chile peppers

15 oz. can chicken broth

2 cloves minced garlic

1 medium yellow onion, finely chopped

2 c. corn (frozen or canned)

1 can black beans (optional)

2 c. water

¼ t. Cayenne pepper

½ t. crushed red pepper flakes

1 t. cumin

1 t. chili powder

1 ½ t. salt

1 t. ground pepper

1 bay leaf

NOTE: Prone to heartburn? Add 1/8 t. baking soda before cooking to neutralize tomato acid. Stir well.

Toppings:

Shredded cheddar cheese

Crumbled tortilla chips and/or warm flour tortillas

Sour cream

Directions:

1. Pull meat off bones of rotisserie chicken and shred or cut into 1" chunks. Place meat in crock pot.

2. Combine canned ingredients in a large blender and blend until smooth. Pour liquid over chicken.

3. Add remaining ingredients to crock pot and stir well.

4. Cook in crock pot on low for 4-6 hours.

5. Remove bay leaf.

6. Serve in bowls topped with shredded cheese, sour cream, and tortilla chips or flour tortillas.

— CHAPTER 5 —

Voices from Beyond

The late winter sun provided a mild 55-degree afternoon, and much of the snow had melted by the time the women finished lunch. After cleaning up, the women walked together to the carriage house. From there Jasmyn and Gwyn set out on an ATV to explore the property together. Lena had a hunch that a set of old skeleton keys she had seen hanging in the kitchen at the carriage house might open the garret on the castle's second floor. Lena took the large iron key ring off the hook and put it in the pocket of her hoodie sweatshirt. As she and Kacie walked back to the castle Lena was acutely aware that her feet were swelling and becoming increasingly painful.

At Kacie's insistence their first stop was the butler's room that Gwyn and Jasmyn had discovered earlier in the day. Being trapped in a dark, forgotten room in a haunted castle was a frightening possibility, so Kacie propped the door open with a heavy upholstered chair from the smoking room in case it decided to slam shut again. The room was just as Gwyn and Jasmyn had described it. Lena tried each of the smaller keys from the ring she found in the carriage house, but none fit the lock on the old black trunk at the foot of the bed. On one side of the trunk Lena noticed faint white stenciled lettering. She brushed off the dust and cobwebs using the sleeve of her sweatshirt.

Squinting in the dim light, Lena read aloud, "C. A. Thomas. Wonder who that was?"

"The butler would be my guess" Kacie said, staring at her cell phone. "I pulled up Wikipedia on my cell phone, and Gwyn was right - those coats in the wardrobe appear to be standard butler attire in the United States for the late 1800s. Let's go see if any of those keys work on that garret upstairs."

Lena's feet were becoming increasingly painful, so much so that she was beginning to think she might need medical attention. As Kacie and Lena emerged from the room, they heard the loud, resonant metal-on-metal sound of the ornate door knocker on the castle's main door. Lena had noticed the magnificent door knocker when she and Jasmyn first arrived at the castle; it was a large brass lion head with a ring gripped in its mouth.

Lena opened the door cautiously. A strikingly handsome, silver-haired Black man in his late 60s stood on the red stone entryway. He wore a long-sleeved royal blue collared shirt tucked neatly into a pair of dark blue jeans and bore a broad, toothy smile. In his left hand he held a toolbox, and a bundle of firewood rested on the ground at his feet.

"Hello there, my name is Calvin. I'm the Panton's handyman – are either of you named Lena?" Lena nodded and extended a hand to the man. Shaking her hand firmly, Calvin explained that he had come to fix a dripping spigot in the greenhouse at Ria's request. Ria had thought it best that he bring some extra firewood to be sure her guests had plenty to keep the castle warm and had asked that he introduce himself before repairing the spigot so he didn't frighten anyone. Lena thanked Calvin for the heads up and welcomed him in.

Calvin placed the firewood next to the fireplace in the foyer. He explained that he had come to know the Panton family in 1984 when his construction company was hired to convert the old carriage house into a resident for James and Ria. After Calvin retired his youngest son, Donald, had taken over leadership of the construction company, but Calvin had personally stayed in touch with the Pantons, handling repairs and minor work at Glen Eyrie Castle. As he turned to leave, he noticed Lena's hobbling stride.

"You hurt, Lena?"

Lena smiled sheepishly. "Not badly, Calvin, but thanks for asking. I'm fine, really." Calvin pulled his wallet out of the back pocket of his jeans and handed a business card to Lena. He told her his eldest son, Will, was a local physician who could probably come by to look at Lena's injury. Lena accepted the card and promised to call if things were not improved the next day, then she thanked Calvin for the firewood and for checking in.

"This place can be scary at times. I have seen and heard my fair share of strange things here. Just call if you need anything at all, you hear?" Lena nodded obediently. Calvin shook her hand and headed back out the front entrance.

Kacie and Lena made their way up the grand staircase and down the long hallway of bedrooms to the strange little door to the second garret. The door was really a half door; the bottom of which was approximately four feet from the floor. Attached to the wall was a rustic, hand-hewn wooden step ladder leading to the door. Since Lena was wearing only cotton socks on her feet, Kacie climbed the ladder and began trying each of the skeleton keys in the lock, but none worked.

Disappointed, Kacie suggested they walk back to the carriage house to see if there were more keys that might work. Kacie and Lena were about ten feet down the hall when the sound of a key turning in a lock stopped them in their tracks. As they turned around, the sound of old hinges groaning loudly filled the corridor. Lena was terrified, but she knew in her gut that the half door had been opened. Huddled together, the two women crept cautiously back to the alcove where the door to the garret was. The door was only slightly open; sticking out of the lock was an old skeleton key.

"My heart is pounding so hard right now," Lena whispered breathlessly.

"Mine, too. Do...do you think it is safe to go in?" Kacie's stammered as she linked her arm with Lena's.

Lena held her right index finger to her lips but did not make a sound. She tugged on Kacie's arm and backed away from the alcove to the room she was staying in, just three doors down the hallway. Lena positioned Kacie in the doorway facing out toward the hallway and told her to keep an eye out for any sign of an intruder.

From her suitcase Lena pulled a small metal box with a combination lock. She opened the box and removed her handgun, a Glock 43. She quickly ejected the magazine and inserted six rounds, then reinserted the magazine.

The familiar clicking noise indicating that the magazine was locked in place garnered Kacie's attention.

Eyes wide, Kacie turned around and stared at Lena in disbelief. "Oh, my God, Lena," Kacie whispered. "A gun? Are you insane? What in the hell are you doing with a gun?"

Lena tucked the gun into the back of the waistband of her jeans and looked at her friend sternly. "I am no one's victim, Kacie. Just in case we are dealing with a person and not a ghost, we need to be able to defend ourselves" she whispered. "Keep your voice down and stay behind me. Let's go."

The two friends walked slowly, quietly back down the hallway, stopping just shy of the alcove. Lena positioned Kacie safely behind her, then removed her gun from her waistband and disengaged the safety. Holding the gun in front of her, she called out loudly "I am armed, and I *will* shoot. Come out now!"

Straining to hear even the slightest sound, the women stood motionless. Hearing nothing, Lena rounded the corner slowly with her gun drawn. Kacie clung to the back of Lena's sweatshirt.

"Come out right now. This is my last warning. I am armed and *will* shoot," Lena shouted assertively.

A frigid breeze rushed at Kacie and Lena, accompanied by a stern female voice that seemed to emanate from the small space between Lena's head and Kacie's. "My dear, that *will not* be necessary." Lena recognized the voice and British accent as that of the brunette woman in the blue dress she had seen in her room that morning.

Stunned silence filled the air as the frigid breeze swirled around the two women. When the air finally stilled Lena lowered the gun, re-engaged the safety, and returned the gun to the back waistband of her jeans. She glanced back at Kacie, and then at the ladder.

"That voice was the woman in the blue dress who was in my room this morning. Same voice, same accent." Lena whispered shakily. "I... I don't believe she is harmful." Lena eyed the half door cautiously, then faced Kacie. "I am going up that ladder. Stay down here until I tell you it is safe to come up, ok?" Kacie nodded hesitantly, intimidated by the idea of being left alone in the hallway.

Lena turned on the flashlight function of her cell phone. She unzipped her hoodie sweatshirt slightly and tucked the phone into her bra for easy access. Disregarding her increasingly painful feet for the moment and emboldened by the suspicion that the woman in the blue dress meant her no harm, Lena climbed the ladder to the fourth step. She removed the cell phone from her bra, shone the flashlight into the darkened room, and leaned in.

Directly in front of Lena was a latch-handled wood door, which she assumed might lead to a closet. To her left was a rough stone wall. The room opened to the right. Because the short door was accessible by a four-foot-high ladder, Lena had expected a low ceiling, but the dark, windowless room was approximately 20 feet long and 15 feet wide with a 10-foot ceiling and wood slat walls. In the far-left corner Lena could see a narrow bed and small side table. A wardrobe sat against the back wall, and a dresser and dressing table with a mirror were positioned against the wall to the right.

Lena noticed that a thick layer of dust covered the floor. She shone the light on the floor looking for footprints in the dust but found it to be undisturbed. She climbed the rest of the way up the ladder and motioned for Kacie to follow.

The narrow bed against the wall was neatly made with a hand-sewn quilt. Lena recognized the pattern on the quilt as Ohio star, a quilting pattern her mother and grandmother had used frequently in their own quilting projects. Lena had one of her grandmother's quilts in her home, and it was a treasured heirloom. Lena remembered her Granny M telling her that the quilt pattern was created in honor of the women and children who had lost their menfolk fighting for the Union in the Civil War.

Though her grandmother had died when Lena was young, she had several fond memories of helping to sort fabrics by shape and color for her grandmother when she was making a quilt for the new baby. Gwyn had been born just a short time afterwards. Their mother had tried to teach Lena and Gwyn to quilt. Gwyn had picked it up quickly and still quilted special occasion gifts. Lena, on the other hand, had no patience for the tedious nature of planning, measuring, cutting, or stitching.

A small object peeking out from under the bed caught Kacie's eye. She strode to the bed, squatted down, and picked the object up. It was a metal comb with a long black wooden handle.

"Interesting old comb," She remarked, handing it to Lena.

Lena inspected the comb for a moment, noting that a number of coarse black hairs were still intertwined in its metal bristles. Setting the comb on the small table beside the bed, Lena remarked, "I think that might be a hot comb – my granny had an electric one. Curly-headed women used them to straighten their hair back in the old days."

Brushing away cobwebs dramatically with her right hand and holding her flashlight with her left hand, Kacie moved toward the old wardrobe. She turned the key that was sticking out of the lock and opened both doors. The old hinges groaned miserably as Kacie pulled the heavy wood doors open. Hanging neatly in the wardrobe were three long black dresses with high collars and three white ruffled Batiste aprons.

"Hot damn! You are not going to believe this Lena – come check this out!" Lena joined Kacie at the wardrobe. The dresses and aprons were exactly like the one worn by the ghostly maid they had seen in the woods earlier that morning. A presence seemed to fill the room as Lena gently touched the ruffle of one of the aprons. The presence did not feel frightening to Lena, but the stillness of the air and the sense that someone other than Kacie and herself was in the room caused her to shiver.

"Well," Lena said softly. "I suppose we know whose room this was. You know what, Kacie? This white apron is exactly like the one I was wearing in my dream last night." She closed the wardrobe doors and turned the key to lock them. Lena remarked that the furnishings of the room were rather nice for maids' quarters, and they were certainly nicer than the furnishings they had seen in the butler's room.

Lena strode to the dressing table and tried to open the drawer, but it did not budge. *Hmmm… she thought, another darned lock without a key.* While

Lena inspected the drawer to the dressing table, Kacie looked through the dresser drawers. She found a single plate, fork, knife, spoon, and tin mug in the top drawer. In the bottom drawer she found an old Bible, a folded knit blanket, and a single skeleton key.

"Lena, was the lock on the trunk in the butler's room brass, by any chance?" Kacie asked as she pocketed the key. Lena nodded, but Kacie did not see the gesture because Lena's cell phone flashlight and Kacie's battery-operated flashlight both died simultaneously.

Bam! The half-door through which they had entered slammed shut, plunging the room into complete darkness. Lena's startled shriek was followed instantly by the sound of the lock turning.

"Oh my God!" Lena exclaimed. "The key was sticking out of the lock on the *outside* of the door! We're trapped!" Kacie followed the sound of Lena's voice, crawling carefully in the darkness until the two bumped heads.

"Ouch!" Lena whispered harshly, squeezing her eyes briefly and rubbing her forehead. With unsteady hands she retrieved a lighter from the front pocket of her jeans and was about to light the flame when she noticed a small, dim ball of light no more than two inches in diameter hovering near the ceiling in the corner of the room above the bed.

"Look, Kacie," she whispered. "Over the bed!" Huddled together in the darkness, Lena and Kacie watched the silvery ball of light dance in the air as it gradually grew to nearly six inches in diameter, casting a soft glow in the room. Lena's heart was beating so loudly she was certain Kacie could hear it.

The orb of light moved slowly to the left, then stopped and hovered beside the latch-handled door across from the half door through which Lena and Kacie had entered. Soft and low, a man's hushed voice spoke. *I hid the truth from my daughters. Now the truth is yours. Open the door and I will show you.*

Fading gradually, the orb disappeared and the room returned to darkness. Lena flicked the lighter, grateful for its dull glow. The women stood up together. Kacie walked over to the small bedside table from which she retrieved an old chamberstick candle holder. She cleared the dust and cobwebs from the candle as best she could and then extended it in Lena's direction. After several attempts the old candle took the flame and Lena returned the lighter to her pocket.

Lena walked to the latch-handled door with great caution, still certain that her beating heart must be audible outside her body. Kacie, holding the candle with both of her trembling hands, followed closely behind, taking care to keep the flame safely distanced from Lena's ponytail. Lena pressed the latch with her thumb and pulled on the door. The old metal hinges screeched loudly as the door opened to reveal exactly what Lena had expected – a closet. To the right of the door inside the closet were three shelves of neatly folded linens. On the back wall of the closet were eight pegs for hanging garments. To the left of the closet door was a long, inverted wooden hanger.

Shocking cool breath on Lena's right ear accompanied directions from the disembodied male voice. *Push! The righthand side under the garment pegs.* Startled by the voice, Kacie drew a sharp breath and took several steps back, nearly dropping the candle holder.

Stepping into the closet, Lena placed both hands under the pegs on the right side of the closet's back wall and gave it a gentle push; to her surprise, it gave way several inches. She pushed again, and as the wall opened to the left Lena realized that the back wall of the closet was a door. The screeching sound of the old metal hinges made Lena cringe as she pushed the door open.

Kacie approached cautiously; by the dim candlelight they could see that the doorway opened to a small stone landing and narrow stone stairway. Masses of heavy cobwebs obscured any view beyond the fourth step. The two agreed that ascending the staircase with only a candle would be a fire hazard given the density of the cobwebs. They pulled the wall of the closet closed, stepped back into the room, and closed the latch-handled door.

Clank. Clink. The distinct clamor of a metal object hitting and then bouncing before finally settling on the wood floor directly behind them caused both women to turn around abruptly. Kacie knelt, using the light of the candle to find the source of the noise. On the floor near the half door was the skeleton key they had used to enter the room. She picked it up and looked at Lena, who's mouth was agape.

"Kacie, I swear to you that key was in the lock on the *outside* of the door! You saw it yourself!" Lena's voice shook as she spoke.

Kacie knelt to take a close look at the half door. "Maybe so, Lena, but it appears this door can be locked either from the inside or the outside!" Kacie inserted the skeleton key into the keyhole.

Kerplunk. Both women breathed a sigh of relief at the sound of the lock turning easily. Soft yellow light from the hallway streamed through the opening door, so Kacie blew out the candle. Lena turned backward and lowered herself down the ladder, grimacing from the pain in her feet. Kacie licked her thumb and forefinger and pinched the candle wick to ensure it was completely extinguished. After returning the candle to the bedside table, Kacie exited the garret. She pulled the half door closed and locked it before handing the skeleton key to Lena and descending the last two steps of the ladder.

"Sweet friend, my nerves are positively shot, and my feet hurt so badly they are throbbing. I am going downstairs to make a strong drink. You with me?" Lena asked. Kacie nodded in agreement and offered Lena her elbow for support. The two started down the hallway and were happy to hear Jasmyn and Gwyn chattering excitedly as they entered the castle foyer, having just returned from their ATV tour of the estate's vast acreage.

Jasmyn helped Kacie make a small pitcher of Mexican mules while Lena settled back into a chair in the main reception hall and Gwyn made a bowl of spicy southwestern cheese dip with tortilla chips. Once a warm fire was going in the fireplace, the women settled into the soft leather chairs to exchange stories while enjoying appetizers and Mexican mules.

"Call me crazy," Jasmyn said after listening quietly for several minutes. "But has anyone else noticed that most of the activity seems to center around Lena? I mean, we have all experienced something. It just seems like Lena is being targeted."

"I'm glad you said something, Jasmyn. I was just thinking the same thing" Gwyn said, savoring a mouthful of dip. She pointed a finger at Kacie and Jasmyn before continuing. "Let's clean up here, then why don't you two go see if that key that Kacie found in the maid's dresser works on the trunk in the butler's room? Lena, there's a stool by the kitchen island – you can sit there and help me get dinner ready." Jasmyn and Kacie nodded in eager agreement.

"Great – I'm haunted. Good to know" Lena exclaimed as she shifted nervously in her chair. She gulped down the remainder of her drink and wiped her mouth with the sleeve of her sweatshirt. "Happy to help in the kitchen, sis. Just put me on a stool and I can be your immobile assistant because my feet are really sore and swollen. What do you have planned for dinner, anyway?"

"You will have to wait and see, but it is going to be the best meal of the weekend," Gwyn replied proudly. "Tonight, we'll need a white or blush wine to go with dinner. Kacie and Jas, you gals grab a couple of bottles from the cellar after you are done in the butler's quarters, ok? Something like an old Chenin Blanc, an aged Condrieu, or a newer Viognier."

Chapter Five Recipes

Mexican Mules

½ c. tequila

4 t. Rose's Sweetened Lime Juice

1 can ginger beer

1 can Sprite

Lime wedges and/or jalapeno slices for garnish

Serve over ice in a copper mug. Drink two.

Beer Cheese Spicy Southwestern Cheese Dip

1 T. butter

½ c. onion, finely diced

1 (32 oz) block of Velveeta, cubed

1 can Ro*Tel® Original Diced Tomatoes & Green Chilies, drained

1 can refried or black beans

1 packet Old El Paso taco seasoning

½ c. milk

¾ c. beer

Directions:

1. Melt butter in a skillet over medium heat

2. Add onions and cook 5 – 7 minutes, stirring occasionally

3. Add beer and simmer an additional 4 minutes

4. Pour into a greased casserole dish.

5. Add milk, cheese, Ro*Tel, and beans.

6. Mix well and cover dish with lid or plastic wrap.

7. Microwave on high stirring every 2 minutes until cheese is melted and ingredients are well-blended.

8. Add milk if needed to thin to desired consistency.

—— CHAPTER 6 ——

Mr. Tall, Cold, and Rusty

Unnerved by the thought of going down into the windowless wine cellar given the events of the day, Kacie refused to go to the wine cellar without a pre-lit lantern and a lighter lest she be trapped in a dark space again. Jasmyn, however, was unphased, so Kacie was happy to follow the eager young woman who practically bounced down the stairs. The dim sconces cast a gloomy light over the grey stone floors and walls, just as they had the evening prior when Kacie had accompanied Lena to the wine cellar.

Jasmyn reached out to open the arched wooden door to the wine cellar, which creaked loudly as it opened. The creak of the cellar door was not new to Kacie, but Jasmyn laughed and commented that the sound was perfect for a haunted castle. Inside the wine room Jasmyn ran her fingers over the metal plaque labels under a row of stone insets containing bottles of red wine along the right wall. Noting that the wine cellar was larger than her parents' living room, she wondered whether she was the first Hispanic person to ever enter the wine cellar.

Kacie headed straight to the large electric cooler for white wines on the back wall, which emitted a low electrical hum. On a shelf labelled "White Burgundy", she found six bottles of 1997 Pouilly Fuisse. She removed two bottles and handed the lantern to Jasmyn. Then she closed the cooler doors and both women turned around to make their way back out of the wine cellar. Both of them stopped in their tracks as they looked toward the open wine cellar door.

There stood the transparent figure of a petite dark-haired woman in a long royal blue dress. The middle-aged woman wore her dark hair in a high, neat chignon with soft curls at the front and at her temples. Her dress had a high neckline, tight bodice, and long sleeves that puffed out at the shoulder and above the elbows but were tight at the forearms and wrists. The gored skirt was long, and tight at the woman's slightly plump waist.

The woman offered them a closed-lip smile and slight bow of the head, and then vanished, leaving nothing but a slight scent of sweet perfume. Jasmyn and Kacie stood still as the temperature in the room quickly lowered, then the sound of delicate heeled footsteps exited the cellar and proceeded up the stairs. Kacie looked at Jasmyn, who stood openmouthed staring at the door, her large brown eyes brimming with tears.

"Eso fue un fantasma," Jasmyn said softly, the lantern shaking in her trembling hand. She looked at Kacie and blinked, allowing tears to escape from her eyes. Overcome with an instinct to comfort the younger woman, Kacie hugged both bottles of wine to her chest with her right hand, and gently took hold of Jasmyn's left arm with the other hand. She guided Jasmyn toward the door and peered out to make sure the large room beyond the wine cellar door was empty.

"I don't have any idea what you just said in Spanish, but you just saw a lady in a long blue dress, right?" Kacie asked. Jasmyn nodded. "OK, then I'm not crazy. I think that might be the same spirit Lena saw in her room this morning. She's gone now - come on, let's go tell Lena and Gwyn." As Kacie and Jasmyn made their way guardedly through the cellar and up the stairs, Kacie wondered which of them was trembling the most.

Gwyn was frying bacon and Lena was chopping fresh, fragrant dill when Jasmyn and Kacie hastened through the batwing doors to the kitchen. Jasmyn's tear-streaked face was expressionless, and Kacie appeared dumbfounded as she led Jasmyn gently by the arm. When Jasmyn saw Lena, she ran to her and threw her right arm around Lena's neck, and then began sobbing.

"Oh, Jas! Sweetie, what is it?" Lena took the lantern from Jasmyn's left hand and set it gently on the counter. Jasmyn's body trembled violently, and she clung to Lena tightly. Between sobs Jasmyn's breaths were sharp and ragged.

Kacie stood motionless just inside the doors with two bottles of wine still clutched to her chest. Gwyn turned off the stove, set the pan on a cool burner, and took the bottles of wine from Kacie, who was pale and expressionless. "Kacie, what happened?" Gwyn asked gently.

"A sp… spirit." Kacie stammered. "Long blue dress. Poufy sleeves. Dark hair in a bu… bun with some curls. She was in the wine cellar. She j.. just smiled and nodded and then she vanished, and we heard footsteps. Jasmyn was talking in Spanish."

Jasmyn sniffled and lifted her head from Lena's shoulder. "Sorry. I do that sometimes. Oh, God, Lena. We saw a ghost. We really did! It was *there* and then it just was *not* there – it disappeared! Like *poof* – gone!"

Gwyn retrieved a frosty bottle of bright yellow liquid from the freezer and two tiny wine glasses from a box on the counter. She filled each glass halfway with the yellow liquid. "Here - this is limoncello. It is made from Everclear, so it is strong." She handed a glass to Kacie and one to Jasmyn. "You can sip it or slam it, but it should help calm your nerves."

Jasmyn drew a deep breath in through her nose and exhaled it slowly through her mouth as she released Lena's shoulders and sat on the stool next to her. Both Kacie and Jasmyn gulped the sweet liquid down quickly. Jasmyn extended her glass to Gwyn who refilled both her glass and Kacie's. Lena handed Jasmyn a paper towel and rubbed her back gently.

Exhausted from their experience and feeling safer in larger numbers, Kacie and Jasmyn decided to stay in the kitchen with Gwyn and Lena to help with dinner preparation rather than try the lock on the trunk in the butler's room. Based on the description of the woman Kacie and Jasmyn had seen in the wine cellar, Lena told the others she felt certain it was the same woman she had seen at the writing desk in her room that morning. She shared that in hindsight the woman had looked familiar to her, but she had not been able to put a finger on exactly why.

"Now that you mention it, Lena, she looked familiar to me, too," Jasmyn said softly as she carried two plates from the kitchen to the dining room. Gwyn followed with two more plates, and Kacie followed with the bottles of wine. Lena lit the lantern on the mantle and joined the others at the table for a feast of cucumber dill salad and pan seared scallops with bacon lemon cream sauce atop a bed of loaded mashed potatoes.

Kacie was raving about dinner when Jasmyn loudly exclaimed, "Oh, I've got it!" For Jasmyn, the sudden realization that she knew exactly who the female spirit was outweighed her anticipation of the first bite of scallop on her fork, which was poised in mid-air. "Oh, my God. It was Queenie!" Kacie looked somewhat annoyed at having been interrupted, but Jasmyn was unphased. "Lena, remember the picture of Queenie from the research packet I made for you? That's the ghost I saw in the wine cellar! She looked just like one of the portraits in the main reception hall."

Lena dropped her fork and covered her mouth, which was full of cucumber salad, with both hands. She hurriedly chewed and swallowed, and then responded "*That's it!* You are right. That's exactly why she looked familiar! But if the woman we saw was Queenie, why did she sign her letter with the initial M?"

"General Panton called her Queenie. It was like a pet name or a nick-name. Her given name was Marie. I remember that from the research I did." Jasmyn smiled knowingly before finally enjoying the first bite of scallop. As she savored the bite, she closed her eyes and declared it the best thing she had ever tasted.

Wondering aloud why she was the only one who had not seen a ghost yet, Gwyn sipped slowly on her wine. Gesturing at Kacie with her fork Gwyn suggested that the maid in Lena's dream, the same one that Lena and Kacie saw in the woods, might be the housemaid, Mitilde, who was mentioned in the letter written by the spirit of Queenie Panton in Lena's room that morning.

Kacie nodded and said she remembered reading in Jasmyn's research that the Pantons had three daughters. Jasmyn nodded affirmatively. Kacie asserted that if the female spirit in the blue dress was Queenie, then the male voice she and Lena heard in the upstairs garret must belong to General Panton since the voice had mentioned keeping a secret from his daughters.

"Now if we can just figure out who Mr. Tall, Cold and Rusty out in the foyer is, we'll be in business," Gwyn proclaimed. Feeling the effects of the wine, the women raised their glasses and toasted the iron knight.

Kacie was feeling overwhelmed by the events of the day, so she suggested that they postpone attempting to unlock the butler's chest and exploring the garret on the second floor until after breakfast Sunday morning. The other women agreed, and together they created a plan for exploring the staircase behind the second-floor garret. The skeleton key to the half door would remain in someone's pocket unless it was being used to lock or unlock a door. That way, even if the door was closed, they would be able to exit the garret safely. They agreed to ascend the staircase in pairs, each pair armed with a broom for cobweb removal and a covered lantern. Jasmyn wanted to be paired with Lena, but only if Kacie and Gwyn would go up the stone stairs first.

"My body produced a lot of adrenaline today," Kacie reflected. "I saw a ghost in the woods, a talking ball of light in the garret, and a woman in the wine cellar. My nerves are a worse wreck than the Titanic, and I am exhausted. Glad I brought some melatonin with me to help me sleep. Y'all want some?"

Lena nodded, and asserted she did not think she should sleep alone. The possibility of sleepwalking again or being woken up by one of the resident spirits had her feeling uneasy, so Gwyn agreed to move to Lena's room. Jasmyn and Kacie decided to again share the blue room they had shared the night before. The two rooms were directly across the hall from one another, so the women could get to each other quickly if necessary. They also agreed to stick together as a group for the remainder of the visit, an agreement which included cleaning up the dinner dishes.

"OK, ladies. Let's get these dishes cleaned up so we can try to relax for a while before bed." Gwyn said as she gathered her plate and wine glass and disappeared into the kitchen.

"Yes, chef!" exclaimed Kacie as she pushed back her chair and picked up her own plate. Lena and Kacie had not yet risen from their chairs yet when the crashing sound of shattering glass rang through the air and Gwyn came barreling back through the batwing doors between the kitchen and dining room. She ran to the back wall of the dining room where she stood wide-eyed facing the kitchen doors, pressing her back and palms to the wall. Gwyn's chest heaved as she struggled to catch her breath.

Kacie looked at Gwyn and then slowly turned to look behind her through the windows of the wooden batwing doors to the kitchen. "Oh, my Lord!" she exclaimed. "That damned knight is standing in the kitchen!"

While Lena and Kacie tended to Gwyn, Jasmyn called Dillon over at the guardhouse. She explained what had happened and asked him to come help her move the knight.

"Again?" Dillon asked. "Yeah, hang on. I'll be right up."

When Dillon arrived, Jasmyn answered the door. After moving the knight back to the foyer, Dillon and Jasmyn chatted for a few minutes while Lena, Gwyn, and Kacie took care of cleaning up the dinner dishes. Dillon said he had an idea that might keep the iron knight in place, but his idea required that he retrieve something from the carriage house. Jasmyn agreed to walk with him. On the short walk to the carriage house the two discussed their favorite bands and discovered they shared a fondness for stand-up comedy.

At the storage barn behind the carriage house, Dillon used his large flashlight to find his way through ATVs, a snowplow, a snowblower, a riding mower and other odds and ends. In the back corner he found what he had been looking for – a bag of salt kept on hand to de-ice the driveway and walkways in the winter.

He pulled a red bandana from inside his coat, placed a couple of handfuls of the salt in the bandana and then tied the ends of the bandana together to form a pouch. Jasmyn looked at him skeptically. Dillon just shrugged, winked, and said he would show her what he had in mind when they got back to the foyer.

Jasmyn felt her cheeks flush; she had only dated Hispanic men before, but she found the young blonde security guard attractive and interesting. On the walk back to the castle, Dillon asked if Jasmyn would be his date for dinner at Margarita at Pine Creek restaurant followed by a show at Loonee's Comedy Corner with some friends the following night. Coyly, Jasmyn replied with a flirtatious wink that she was inclined to say yes but needed to be impressed with whatever his plan was for keeping the iron knight in place before making up her mind.

Dillon and Jasmyn were laughing when they entered the main castle door. Lena, Kacie, and Gwyn met them in the foyer, interested to see what Dillon's solution might be for the wandering knight, whom they had officially decided must be referred to as "Mr. Tall, Cold & Rusty." Dillon laughed at the name.

He got down on his hands and knees, opened the bandana and sprinkled the salt in a circle around the knight. Jasmyn admired Dillon's body, watching his muscular shoulders as he used all the salt, taking great care that there was no break in the circle. Lena nudged Jasmyn gently and shot her a knowing smile. Suddenly feeling feverish and weak, Lena lowered herself onto the hearth of the fireplace in the foyer.

"I saw this trick during a cemetery tour in Louisiana a couple of years ago" Dillon said as he stood up and brushed the salt off his navy blue uniform slacks. "Southerners say a ghost can't cross a salt line." Jasmyn eyed Dillon cynically, but Lena, Gwyn, and Kacie nodded affirmatively.

"So, Jasmyn, are you impressed enough?" Dillon asked, looking at Jasmyn with a boyish grin.

"*Very* clever," she mused, placing a finger on her chin as she feigned deliberation. "Your creativity *is* compelling. Yes, I think I am impressed enough to go out with you tomorrow night."

Dillon tucked the bandana back into his coat. "Great – we'll have a blast. I will pick you up here at 5:45 tomorrow. Goodnight, everyone." As he opened the door to leave Dillon pointed sternly at the knight and firmly said, "Now you stay put, Rusty," before pulling the door closed behind him.

Jasmyn walked to the door and locked it. Smiling, she turned around to see Lena, Kacie, and Gwyn all staring at her with amusement. "What? Why are you all staring at me?"

Lena cleared her throat, crossed her arms, and smirked. "Well, look at little miss Jasmyn flirt! Does a certain young lady have something she would like to share?"

"Well, apparently I have a date tomorrow with a *really* cute security guard," Jasmyn said bashfully. Her smile faded, though, as she confessed that she had not brought clothing suitable to wear on a date.

Lena knew that Jasmyn had limited financial resources, so she said "I was just thinking that I need something a bit more appropriate than jeans to wear on Monday when I meet with the assessor. Besides, Jasmyn, you've been a wonderful intern and I would love to buy you something special as a thank you for all of your hard work."

Lena had made an appointment with the secretary of the board of directors for the Old Colorado City History Center Museum for the following day, so she suggested that Gwyn and Kacie take that appointment to learn more about Glen Eyrie Castle and the Pantons while she and Jasmyn visited a couple of the nearby boutiques.

Jasmyn shook her head. "No, Lena. My parents would not want me taking advantage of you but thank you for the offer. You really are a generous person."

Lena smiled fondly at the young intern. "I would have felt the same way at your age. But you are a grown woman, Jasmyn. It is a good time for you to learn the difference between taking advantage of someone and accepting a gift. Now, unless you want bags under your eyes for your big date, I think we all need to try to get some sleep. Kacie, I am positive that I have a fever. Can I have some of your melatonin and ibuprofen?"

Before settling into bed Lena and Gwyn took turns showering. They left the bathroom door open, and Lena insisted on lighting the lantern in the bedroom as well as the pillar candle in the bathroom in case the lights went out. She confided in her younger sister that she was afraid to turn out the lights. Since being trapped in the darkness in the garret that afternoon, the idea of sleeping in the dark terrified Lena. They agreed to sleep with the bathroom light on and the door cracked.

Jasmyn loaned Lena some CBD-infused oil to rub on her raw feet. Lena showed her feet to Gwyn; they were badly bruised, and the skin surrounding the cuts was red and warm to the touch. Walking even a few steps had become increasingly painful, and Lena expressed concern about the possibility of sleepwalking again.

Gwyn furrowed her brow, uneasy about the condition of Lena's feet. She felt her sister's forehead and confirmed that Lena seemed to be running a fever. Gwyn insisted that reaching out to the handyman's doctor son would be wise if Lena's condition was not substantially improved the next morning.

In the meantime, the sisters decided it would be best to move the writing desk in front of the door to prevent Lena from exiting the bedroom without making enough noise to awaken Gwyn, who was a notoriously heavy sleeper. While Gwyn settled into the lounge chair near the window to read her book, Lena propped herself up in the bed. She spent a while writing in her journal about the day's events, then turned off the lamp on her nightstand table and closed her eyes. Comforted by the bathroom light and her sister's presence, Lena slept soundly. Unfortunately, her sister was not as fortunate.

Chapter Six Recipes

Cucumber Dill Salad

   2 English cucumbers, sliced
   ½ white onion, sliced
   1 t. dried dill weed
   ½ t. salt
   ½ t. pepper
   ½ c. white vinegar
   ½ c. hot water
   ½ c. sugar

Directions:

Combine vinegar, sugar, dill, salt, pepper, and hot water. Stir until sugar is dissolved. Add cucumber and onion slices. Ensure that cucumbers and onions are covered with the liquid, then cover and place in the refrigerator for several hours. Serve chilled.

Loaded Mashed Potatoes

   3 ½ lbs. Yukon gold potatoes
   1 c. heavy whipping cream
   8 oz. room temperature cream cheese, cubed
   ¼ c. sour cream
   10 T. salted butter.
   4 t. minced garlic
   1 ½ t. pepper
   1 ½ t. salt
   Zest of one lemon
   8 slices bacon, cooked and chopped

Directions:

1. Peel potatoes and cut into 1" cubes

2. Bring a large pot of water to a slow boil and add potatoes.

3. Simmer until fork tender (approx. 20 minutes)

4. While potatoes are simmering, melt 1 T. of butter in a saucepan.

   - When melted, add minced garlic, and cook over medium heat for two minutes, stirring frequently.

   - Add remaining butter, cream, lemon zest, salt, and pepper.

   - When butter is melted add cream cheese and turn burner to low setting. Stir occasionally.

5. When potatoes are done, drain them and put them into a large mixing bowl.

6. Add sour cream to potatoes, then pour the saucepan mixture over the potatoes.

7. Mix with a handheld mixer on medium-low speed until potatoes are desired consistency.

8. Fold in bacon bits and serve warm.

Pan Seared Scallops with Bacon Lemon Cream Sauce

16-20 large room-temperature scallops, dried with a paper towel
Salt and pepper to taste
8 slices bacon, cooked and chopped
3 T. butter
2 T. all-purpose flour
4 c. heavy cream
1 ½ c. grated Parmesan cheese
2 lemons, juiced and zested
Chopped chives for garnish

Directions:

1. Allow scallops to come to room temperature, then dry with paper towels and season lightly with salt and pepper.

2. After cooking bacon in a medium skillet, remove bacon and set aside on a paper towel to cool.

3. In the skillet with bacon grease, add 2 T. flour and whisk over medium heat to make a roux.

4. When roux begins to thicken, add cream, Parmesan, and lemon zest to the skillet and blend well with a whisk.

5. Reduce the sauce over medium heat by half, and then stir in half of the cooked bacon. Reduce heat to low to keep warm.

6. In a separate skillet, melt the butter over medium high heat.

7. When the butter is melted and the skillet is hot, add scallops.

8. Sear the scallops for 1½ - 2 minutes without moving them until a nice brown sear develops.

9. Turn the scallops over and add lemon juice; cook for 1 minute then remove scallops from pan, set aside.

10. Plate scallops browned side up atop loaded mashed potatoes (recipe above) and top each scallop with some of the remaining bacon crumbles.

11. Drizzle scallops with sauce.

12. Top with chives.

— CHAPTER 7 —

Out of Commission

"Wake up sleeping beauty because I've got some serious shit to tell you about." Lena opened one eye and glared at Gwyn, who was shaking her shoulder.

"Hey, cut it out! Let me sleep," Lena whined, covering her head with her pillow. She was hot and dizzy.

"No way, girlie," Gwyn said, yanking the pillow away and gesturing toward a steaming cup of coffee on the bedside table. "It is 9:00, and we have a busy day ahead of us."

Lena rubbed the sleep from her eyes and sat up. Her feet were throbbing, and her face was warm. What she really wanted to do was go back to sleep, but Gwyn was clearly agitated and insisted that Lena sit up.

Savoring a sip of coffee, Lena scowled as Gwyn opened the curtains, allowing the bright morning sun to flood the room with light. Squinting at her sister while her eyes adjusted to the daylight, Lena asked, "What is the serious shit you want to tell me, and why did you have to open the curtains? Rude! And by the way, you look as awful as I feel. You ok?"

"No, ma'am I am not okay. It was a very rough night, and I am tired and hungry!" Gwyn snapped. "Kacie is up and ready, too, so she is going to help me get breakfast ready. Jasmyn is across the hall getting ready. She is scared and wants both bedroom doors open. She said there were red flowers on the bedspread when she and Kacie woke up this morning. Get dressed and come downstairs. There is no need to get made up since we are headed into the garret. I will tell you everything at breakfast."

Lena felt weak and feverish, and her feet hurt so badly that bearing weight was almost more pain than she could handle. She managed to put on a pair of leggings, a sweatshirt, and a baseball cap. She was washing her feet gently with a warm washcloth when she noticed numerous blisters and red streaks on the bottom of her feet.

When Jasmyn entered the room, she inspected Lena's feet. She wondered whether the blisters, red streaks, and warmth might be indicative of a possible infection. Lena agreed that calling Calvin's son would be wise. Jasmyn and Lena agreed that clean socks and Lena's rubber-soled bedroom slippers were the best solution for Lena's feet for the time being.

Lena hobbled gingerly to the small elevator at the end of the hall. When the elevator opened on the first floor Lena shuffled to the dining room with Jasmyn's assistance, grimacing with each painful step. By the time she reached the dining room, tears were streaming down her face and she had broken into a sweat. She reached into the pocket of her sweatshirt and pulled out Calvin's card, which she handed to Kacie.

"Something is very wrong, Kacie. I'm in tremendous pain and I am burning up. Please call Calvin's son." With what seemed like her last ounce of strength, Lena angled her chair and slowly lifted each leg onto the chair next to her. Kacie felt Lena's forehead, then removed the socks from Lena's feet and inspected them carefully. Frowning with concern, Kacie hurried to the main castle foyer where cell phone reception was better. She called Calvin who promised to have his son, Will, call Kacie back. Meanwhile, Jasmyn fetched a pillow to place under Lena's feet and told Lena about the red flowers that had mysteriously appeared in her room overnight. She was certain they were the same kind of flower the knight had been holding when Kacie and Gwyn had arrived at the castle Friday afternoon.

Gwyn emerged from the kitchen with a tray of freshly made cranberry scones; Kacie followed behind with a pot of fresh coffee and two ibuprofen tablets, which she handed to Lena. "Calvin's son, Will, is on duty at the hospital right now, but Calvin is going to have him call my number as soon as he gets a free minute. Lena, one way or another you are definitely in need of medical attention this morning."

Lena nodded and thanked Kacie for the ibuprofen. "Gwyn," Lena said, reaching over to touch her sister's hand. "You said it was a rough night. Why don't you tell us about it?"

"Okay, but you are going to think I've lost my mind" Gwyn said. She shook her head and took a deep breath. "I was sound asleep but woke up because the room was really cold. I pulled the covers up over my shoulders but could not shake the feeling that someone... or some*thing*... was staring at me, so I opened my eyes. There was a man sitting in the upholstered chair in the corner of the room! He was sort of glowing, and I could see through him. I tried to wake you up, Lena, I was shaking you, but you would not move."

Gwyn shot her sister a frustrated look. "I looked back up at the man, and I really was hoping he would be gone, but he was still there. He put a finger up to his lips, and I kid you not - he *shushed me*! Then he started to... like... fade and I heard his voice say, *'Don't be scared, Gwyn, I am here to help. Let your sister sleep for now, but tomorrow you must take her to a doctor. The rest can wait.'* I looked over at you, and when I looked back at the man, he was gone. The chair was just empty – there was no sign of him!"

Gwyn shook her head again and stared into her coffee cup, then continued. "That is all I remember – I thought maybe it was a dream, but it wasn't because I am positive it was real. I know I saw that man sitting in that chair! Well, most of him anyways – his legs sort of disappeared below the knees. He was obviously from a long time ago, too. He had short hair parted on the side – it was brown and curly, and he had a moustache that curled up at the ends. He was wearing an old-fashioned brown suit – it looked like wool. Pants, short-waisted jacket, and a matching vest underneath. Under the vest he had on a white shirt and a tie. The collar on the shirt was weird – the corners sort of poked out above the tie. He was really distinguished looking, and he had a cane in one hand. God, Lena – *he called me by my name!*"

Gwyn raised a trembling hand and pointed at her sister. She continued in a voice so hushed that the other women leaned in slightly to hear her. "That is why I woke you up this morning – you were so still I thought maybe you were… well, it doesn't matter." Gwyn squeezed Lena's hand and took a sip of coffee. Jasmyn started to say something, but Gwyn held up her palm and stopped her.

"That is not all that happened. The next thing I knew, I was waking up because the room was cold again – so cold I was shivering. I could feel someone standing beside me next to the bed and I knew if I opened my eyes, I was not going to like what I saw, so I stayed still and pretended to be asleep. But then I felt this freezing cold hand on my arm, and I heard somebody whisper, '*Wake up!*' I opened my eyes and there was a girl with long brown hair and bangs in a white dress standing in front of me."

Pointing toward the door between the dining room and the main reception hall, Gwyn continued. "As God is my witness, I am telling you it was the same long-haired girl in that great big portrait on the wall opposite the fireplace in the main reception hall! I am talking about the portrait to the left of Queenie's portrait. Then, get this - her lips never moved, but she still talked to me. She said her father wanted the truth to be known. She said she knew the truth and had hidden it according to his instructions when he was dying. Then she said, '*The key and the Bible from Mitilde's dresser will lead you to the truth,*' and just disappeared! The next thing I knew the little asshole birds chirping outside woke me up and I felt like I had hardly slept."

Just then Kacie's cell phone vibrated loudly. "Kacie Whitmore," Kacie said into the phone as she answered the call. "Oh, Dr. Winslow, thank you for calling me back." Kacie put her phone on speaker so she and Lena could speak with the doctor while Jasmyn helped Gwyn tidy up the breakfast dishes.

Jasmyn felt certain that the man Gwyn had seen must have been General Wynston Jamison Panton. Gwyn said both ghosts had terrified her, though she sensed that neither ghost intended to harm or frighten her. She had the feeling that their messages were important and that there was an urgency about the messages. Jasmyn suggested that Gwyn snap a picture of the portrait in the main hall and see if the secretary of the board of directors for the Old Colorado City History Center Museum might be able to tell her who it was. Gwyn agreed, and the two walked to the reception hall together and took a picture of the portrait with Gwyn's cell phone.

Dr. Winslow felt that Lena should be seen in the emergency room as soon as possible, but Lena knew she could not possibly make it out the foyer, down the stone steps, over the small bridge and to the car. She also knew that pressing on the gas pedal would be excruciating, so she could not drive. On top of everything, Lena's legs had begun aching all the way up to her knees. She was weak, nauseous, and had chills. Kacie called the guard shack to see if the guard on duty might be able to help get Lena to the car.

Alejandro Gonzales was the guard on duty. At 54 years old, he was a retired police officer and an avid hiker in excellent physical condition. He took one look at Lena and knew she needed medical attention, so he attempted to convince Lena that calling an ambulance was the prudent thing to do. Lena refused, so Alejandro reluctantly agreed to give her a piggyback ride to Gwyn's car instead. Once she was in the passenger seat Lena gave Jasmyn a $100 bill and made her promise to buy something nice for her date. Then she handed her car keys to Kacie.

Closing her eyes and wishing the nausea away, Lena fastened her seatbelt while Gwyn entered the address for the University of Colorado Health Memorial Hospital into the navigation system. Lena tried to open her eyes again, but her head swam with dizziness and there was nothing but sickening darkness. She felt herself helplessly sinking deeper and deeper as if she was swirling down a drain until the darkness took her completely over.

Beep. Beep. Beep. Beep. Beep. A faint, incessant beeping sound brought Lena out of the darkness. Aware of a weight on her face, she reached for it, but someone caught her hand and laid it gently to her side. She struggled to open her eyes. When they finally opened, she found herself in a hospital bed facing a smiling red-haired woman in purple scrubs. The woman was holding a clip board.

"Ms. Thomas, my name is Martha. You are in a surgical recovery room at UC Health Hospital in Colorado Springs. Do you understand?" Lena's felt as though her head weighed 100 pounds, but she managed to nod slightly. "Good," said Martha. "It is normal to feel sluggish after anesthesia. I need you to leave the oxygen mask on your face, please." Martha adjusted something on an IV bag, jotted a note on her clipboard, and opened the peach-colored curtain wall. "Your sister and friends are in the waiting room. You rest, and I'll go let them and the doctor know that you are awake."

After several long, laborious blinks, Lena looked drowsily at her feet; they protruded from the blanket that covered the rest of her body and were heavily bandaged with sterile gauze. Her eyes followed the beeping sound to its source - a heart monitor. She noticed an IV in her right hand and a pulse oximeter on her right forefinger. She wiggled her fingers slightly just to be sure she could. Reassured by the knowledge that Gwyn and Kacie were nearby, she closed her eyes and felt them roll back in her head. Rather than fight them she drifted off to sleep.

A squeezing sensation on her left bicep brought Lena back out of her slumber. She turned her head to the left and opened her eyes. The nurse in the purple scrubs was standing beside her bed watching an electronic blood pressure machine. The cuff released its hold on her bicep and Martha made another note on her clipboard. She placed a gentle hand on Lena's shoulder.

"Hello, Selena. Nice to see you waking up. I would like to adjust the bed and prop you up a bit. Would that be alright with you?" Lena nodded. Martha set down the clipboard and walked to the right side of Lena's bed. Using controls that Lena could not see, she raised the head of Lena's bed and then adjusted the pillow under her neck.

"Thank you," Lena croaked. Realizing her throat was sore Lena placed her right hand on her throat.

Martha moved a wheeled tray to the bed and positioned the tray over Lena's lap. "The breathing tube can leave your throat sore. Here is a bowl of ice chips for you to suck on when you feel up to it. Your sister is waiting to see you. May I bring her in?" Lena nodded drowsily. Now that her head felt clearer, she was aware of where she was and the reason she was in Colorado Springs.

Moments later Gwyn entered. "Hey big sister," she said, pulling the curtain closed behind her. Gwyn planted a kiss on Lena's forehead.

"Hey," Lena said hoarsely. She reached for the spoon in the Styrofoam bowl, pulled the oxygen mask down, and put a few small pieces of crushed ice in her mouth. "What happened?"

Gwyn put the oxygen mask back over Lena's mouth and nose. Then she pulled a chair up to the left side of Lena's bed, sat down, lifted Lena's left hand, and placed it in her own. "You passed out in the passenger seat before I put the car into drive, Lena. The security guard called an ambulance and kept your head straight to keep your airway open until the paramedics arrived. You really scared the heck out of us. Your temperature was 103 degrees when you got here."

The peach curtain opened again, and a doctor wearing a white coat over blue scrubs entered the room. Nurse Martha followed closely behind him. The doctor was a light-skinned Black man with green eyes and a strong, square jawline. His brown hair was lighter in color and less coarse than that of most Black men; it was longer on the top, but short and sharp on the sides. He rolled a stool up next to her bed and sat down.

"Hi Ms. Thomas, I am Dr. Will Winslow. I believe you have met my dad, Calvin. May I have your permission to discuss your medical condition with your sister in the room?" Lena nodded. "Your sister tells me you went sleepwalking barefoot in the snow up at Glen Eyrie Castle Friday night. Have you ever sleepwalked before?"

Lena shook her head. "No, never." She placed her hand on her stomach as a wave of heat and nausea swept over her. "I feel nauseous." Martha retrieved a pink container from a drawer beside the bed and handed it to her. Lena supposed it would be better to try to catch her vomit in the pink bowl than it would be to spew it all over the handsome doctor.

"Do pain medications typically upset your stomach, Ms. Thomas?" the doctor asked.

"Yes. I don't take them for that reason" Lena replied faintly. "Please call me Lena." Somehow just moving her head and speaking seemed to be more physically demanding than anything Lena had done recently. She swallowed, desperately hoping the nausea would subside.

Dr. Winslow scribbled something on the clipboard and directed Martha to order some substances Lena had never heard of. "Lena, we're going to give you some anti-nausea medicine through your IV. That should alleviate the nausea quickly. I have also ordered a small patch for Martha to place behind your ear. It will prevent nausea for a couple of days. Do you understand?" Lena nodded.

"Ms. Thomas, you have second-degree frost bite on several toes and on the bottom of both feet. That is what caused the soles of your feet to blister. Unfortunately, you have also developed an infection from the abrasions on your feet. That infection progressed into an unusually aggressive bacterial infection called sepsis. Have you heard of sepsis before?" Lena nodded again.

"Sepsis is the body's overreaction to infection. It can lead to tissue damage, organ failure, or even death. Normally sepsis does not set in for several days. In fact, I have never seen such a rapid onset before. You are fortunate that you got to the hospital when you did. We drained the blisters and removed some infected tissue from the bottom of your feet to try and stop the infection from spreading. You have more than two dozen stitches in the bottom of your feet so try not to stretch, okay?"

Though her mind was foggy and sluggish, Lena's heart raced, and her breathing was faster than normal. She struggled to maintain focus on Dr. Winslow as he spoke. "We have you on a strong antibiotic and pain medication, as well as oxygen and IV fluids to maintain blood flow and oxygen to your organs."

Martha returned to the room with a syringe and a small square silver packet. Lena's vision began to blur as she watched Martha empty the syringe into her IV drip line. The nurse cleaned behind Lena's right ear with an alcohol swab, opened the silver packet and placed something cool on the cleaned patch of skin. Lena closed her eyes, aware that the doctor was still talking to her, but she did not have the energy to open her eyes back up. Helpless to reopen her eyes, Lena surrendered back into the darkness.

When she awoke her eyelids felt so heavy that opening them was a physical struggle. Through long, labored blinks Lena could discern that she was in a different room, and a nurse was busying herself with something next to Lena's bed. The oxygen mask still covered Lena's mouth and nose, and the familiar beeping of the heart monitor offered reassurance that she was still alive as she drifted in and out of sleep.

The sound of scissors cutting through something and slight pressure on her right foot brought Lena back out of sleep. She moved her head and opened her eyes enough to see Dr. Winslow and a nurse in pink scrubs at the foot of her bed, both wearing masks that covered their mouths and noses. The doctor gently pulled the gauze bandages off and studied the bottom of her right foot.

"Hi Lena," Dr. Winslow said, smiling at her. "We are just checking on things and changing your bandages. This is Carol, she is an intensive care nurse and will be taking care of you overnight." Lena wanted to speak, but did not have the energy, so she offered a slight nod instead. The nurse cut through the bandages on her left foot for Dr. Winslow, who gently removed the gauze, lifted her foot, and studied it thoughtfully. He then nodded at the nurse, removed the gloves from his hands, and pulled a chair up beside Lena's bed.

"Things look good, Lena, and your fever is coming down nicely. You are making good progress already." He smiled at her warmly, and Lena winced as the nurse rubbed something that felt like Vaseline onto the bottom of her tender feet. She figured the bottom of her feet must look like raw meat.

Dr. Winslow shone a light into her eyes and squeezed several of her fingernails, then jotted some notes. "Your sister and friends have been waiting for you to wake up so they can see you. If you think you are up for it, I will allow them to come in for a few minutes once Carol is done bandaging your feet. Would you like that?" Lena nodded. She tried to push herself up with her arms, but quickly realized she lacked the strength.

Dr. Winslow put a gentle hand on her shoulder. "Ms. Thomas, please do not try to do much of anything. Let us do things for you, at least for now. Carol will help you get comfortable. My colleague, Dr. Chen will be on duty for the next 12 hours, and I will be back tomorrow." When the handsome doctor exited through the door, Lena caught a glimpse of the maid from the woods standing in the hall, though she vanished as the doctor walked right through her.

After Carol was done bandaging Lena's feet, she raised the head of the bed and propped Lena comfortably with several pillows. Then she left the room. She returned with Gwyn, Kacie, and Jasmyn in tow, each wearing a mask. "Just ten minutes, and please do your best to keep her still and calm," Carol said firmly. "I will be right outside if you need anything."

Jasmyn looked sporty and chic in a low messy bun, skinny jeans, a white V-neck tee, violet-red blazer, and ankle boots. Lena remembered that the intern had a date with the security guard, so she offered the young woman a thumbs up. Jasmyn told Lena that she had called the human resources office at Chamberlain International Realty, and that they were sending an associate to Colorado Springs to help Jasmyn handle the meeting at Glen Eyrie with the assessor the following day.

Appearing tired, or perhaps stressed, Gwyn said Calvin had called Ria and explained the situation, so Ria insisted the women stay at Glen Eyrie for as long as they needed. Gwyn was in communication with David and Ria via text and had spoken at length with Ben over the phone. Kacie said something about a blizzard, but once again Lena lost the battle with her eyelids and surrendered to the dark, empty sleep that beckoned her.

Chapter Seven Recipes

Cranberry scones

1 orange, zested and juiced
1 1/4 c. flour
1/3 c. sugar
1 ½ t. baking powder
¼ t. cinnamon
1 t. almond extract
¼ c. butter, chilled
3 T. half and half or whole milk
1 egg, beaten
2/3 c. dried cranberries, quartered
Penzey's ® Vanilla Sugar

Directions:

1. In a mixing bowl combine flour, sugar, cinnamon, baking powder and salt. Cut in the butter until the contents are crumbly.

2. In a separate bowl, combine half and half (or milk), almond extract, 1 T. juice from the orange, orange zest, and 2 tablespoons beaten egg; add to crumb mixture just until moistened.

3. Stir in dried cranberries.

4. Knead gently on a floured surface, then press dough into a greased 6" round cake pan.

5. Cut dough into eight wedges and place each wedge on a plate lined with waxed paper.

6. Chill in refrigerator for 45 minutes.

7. Preheat oven to 425 degrees

8. Place chilled wedges on a cookie sheet lined with parchment paper.

9. Brush with remaining egg mixture and sprinkle liberally with vanilla sugar.

10. Bake until golden (13-15 minutes).

— CHAPTER 8 —

The Butler's Secret

Aside from the hourly squeeze from the electric blood pressure cuff and occasional prods and sounds from the nurse, Lena slept soundly for nearly 18 hours. When she awoke her eyes opened easily, and her mind felt clearer than it had the day before. Lena was not sure what day it was and realized that much of her recent memory was a confusing blur. She stretched instinctively, but the resulting pain in her feet caused her to recoil quickly. She pulled the oxygen mask off her face, which set off a dull alarm. Lena rolled onto her side, curled into a ball, and wept.

A plump nurse with a short grey bob haircut entered and pressed a button on the wall. She helped Lena to sit up, raised the head of the bed and arranged two pillows behind Lena's head and neck. As the nurse gently washed Lena's face with a cool wet washcloth, she introduced herself as Barbie and asked Lena to describe her pain on a scale of one to ten.

"Eight," Lena whispered. "I feel really weak and shaky. And emotional – I do not know why I am crying. I do not know what day it is. I am so scared."

A second nurse entered the room and confirmed that the med cart was just down the hall. "Things ok here?" she asked. Barbie nodded and sent the younger nurse to fetch a cannula and a bland breakfast tray.

"You cry if you need to cry, Miss Thomas." Barbie said gently. "Your body has been through a lot and you have a whole lot of medicine coursing through your system. After the med cart comes and you eat something, you will feel better. Then we will get you a bath." Lena nodded gratefully. A bath did sound nice, though she was suspicious about what a bath in the intensive care unit might entail. Barbie placed a box of facial tissue on Lena's lap, patted her hand and promised to return shortly.

A man in scrubs pushing a cart of medicines arrived. He had Lena lay her head back on the pillow and told her to expect some light headedness. He emptied a syringe into her IV line, hung a new IV bag, checked her IV lines, and drew some blood. Lena's head swam so she held onto the bed rails as if that might stop the room from shifting around her. Barbie returned to the room and encouraged Lena to rest her head back on the pillows, assuring her that the sensation would pass quickly.

"Dilaudid does a number on your equilibrium, but it is the most effective medication for pain. Now that you are up, let's get rid of the oxygen mask. Does that sound alright, Ms. Thomas?" Barbie asked. "Your numbers look good, so I think we can switch you over to a cannula." Barbie removed the oxygen mask from Lena's face and placed two small plastic prongs in Lena's nostrils as Gwyn entered the room. The lightweight tube to which the prongs were attached was less obtrusive and much more comfortable than the oxygen mask had been.

A nurse arrived with a tray of eggs, green gelatin, toast, and a cup of ice. Barbie propped Lena up further and promised that having some food in her stomach would help Lena feel stronger and more in control of her body. After determining that the Dilaudid-induced dizziness had subsided, Barbie reminded Gwyn to keep Lena still and calm, and then left the room.

While Lena eyed the eggs and toast with disinterest, Gwyn told her that Jasmyn would be driving back to Denver with the Chamberlain International Realty representative once the appointment with the assessor was finished. Mid-term exams were coming up, and the intern needed to get back to classes. Gwyn filled in Lena's memory, and told her it was Monday morning. Kacie was at the library following up on some information that the secretary of the board of directors for the Old Colorado City History Center Museum had given her.

Gwyn was excited to share with Lena that the secretary had confirmed the brunette in the white dress whose portrait hung in the main reception hall was General Wynston Jamison Panton's eldest daughter, Evalynn. General Panton's daughters had inherited the castle after their father passed but married affluent men and had no apparent need for the castle. The daughters had tried to gift Glen Eyrie to the city of Colorado Springs, but the city had declined the gift due to fears pertaining to the cost of maintenance and property taxes. Evalynn and her husband lived in the castle for many years and raised their children there.

Though Lena was having difficulty comprehending as fast as Gwyn was speaking, her sister's presence helped her feel more at ease. Dr. Winslow stopped by and said that if Lena continued to improve, she would be moved out of intensive care, possibly that evening. Lena told him that she felt weak, shaky, and anxious. He assured Lena that feeling jittery was nothing to be concerned about but ordered a sedative to help calm her down.

Though skeptical, Dr. Winslow was intrigued by Gwyn's stories about the strange occurrences at Glen Eyrie, so he stayed and chatted for several minutes. He said his father, Calvin, claimed to have encountered spirits at Glen Eyrie. Before leaving to continue his rounds, he encouraged Lena to try to eat something and to pay particular attention to drinking liquids. He then reminded her to call the nurse if she needed more pain medicine. Lena gave the doctor a thumbs up and watched him leave the room, wishing through the haze of the medications that the man was not wearing a long white doctor's coat over his scrubs.

When Barbie returned announcing it was time for a bath, Gwyn left to get some lunch. Lena felt much better after the bed bath, though her body continued to tremble. Lena disliked feeling so out of control of her body. She wiped frustrated tears from her face, prompting Barbie to bring her a box of tissues.

"The doctor approved a mild sedative for you," Barbie said as she emptied a syringe of liquid into Lena's IV line. "Sleeping more than usual is a good thing right now because sleep helps your body build up its immune system and fight off bacteria. But honey, you have got to eat something." Barbie stayed with Lena until she stopped trembling. When Lena confirmed that she felt tired and relaxed, Barbie turned out the light and left. Ignoring the crackers Barbie had left for her, Lena closed her eyes and again surrendered to sleep.

Clickety clack. Clickety clack. Clickety clack. Lena awoke to the sound of Gwyn typing on her laptop computer. The clock on the wall read 4:10, and Lena figured she had not been awake for more than an hour all day. She felt sleepy and peaceful, and her body was no longer shaking.

"Is it still Monday?" she asked with a raspy voice.

Gwyn stopped typing and looked at her sister. "Well, hi there," Gwyn said. "Yes, it is late Monday afternoon. There is a wicked winter storm forecasted; in fact, it is already snowing, so I will need to head out before too long. How are you feeling?"

Lena smiled. "Like a drug addict whose feet went through a meat grinder. My throat is so dry – will you please ask if I can have something to drink?" Gwyn nodded and headed to the nurses' station. She returned with Barbie carrying a small tub that contained a purple popsicle, a cup of ice, a lemon-lime soda, and a bottled water. Barbie helped Lena sit up again and told her that her white cell count had dropped, which meant the infection was responding well to the antibiotics. Lena told the nurse she felt better, but that her feet were beginning to throb again.

"Med cart will be here at 6:00, but I can bring you some acetaminophen now," Barbie said. "Ms. Thomas, we'd like to see you eat something substantive. If you can do that, Dr. Winslow has a regular room on the fourth floor ready for you. Tonight, we have chicken noodle or turkey and rice soup on the dinner menu. What sounds good?" Though she did not have an appetite, Lena found the possibility of a quieter room with less frequent check-ins from the nurses appealing, so she chose the chicken noodle soup.

After a throat-soothing bite of popsicle, Lena told Gwyn she had seen Mitilde in the hallway at the hospital. Gwyn was not surprised and said that the maid had come to her in a dream and told Gwyn that she was watching over Lena. Gwyn claimed the castle had been quiet the prior night, aside from the sound of footsteps in the hallway at 1:15 a.m., but that had turned out to be Jasmyn returning from her date with Dillon. The women had risen early and readied the castle for the assessor. Then Gwyn and Kacie had gone to brunch and then gone their separate ways, having planned to meet at the hospital around 5:00.

"Lena, are you clear-headed enough right now to understand something important?" Gwyn's expression was serious.

"I'm not sure, Gwyn, but I can try," Lena replied as a nurse arrived with a dinner tray. With arms that felt like dead weights, she opened the can of soda and took the two acetaminophen tablets from the tiny paper cup. Noticing that her head still felt too heavy for her neck, Lena rested her head back on the pillows.

"Lena Thomas, you will eat two bites of that soup before I tell you anything." Gwyn said, snatching the popsicle from Lena's grasp. "And what I have to tell you is guaranteed to blow your mind!" Gwyn folded her arms, sat back in her chair, and gave her sister a stern look.

The smell of the soup was unappealing to Lena, but she discovered that the warm liquid felt good on her throat. While Lena sipped at the warm, tasteless broth, Gwyn told her that although she and Kacie had not had time to explore the staircase in the garret on the second floor, they had taken the skeleton key from the maid's dresser to the butler's room. The key successfully unlocked the trunk, which contained Charles' diary and a letter.

"I read the diary today," Gwyn said. "The diary begins on May 7, 1895 and ends on June 7, 1895. You should read it when you feel up to it but let me tell you about it in a nutshell. Charles grew up in an orphanage; the only family he had was a sister, and he had no work skills to speak of. He aged out of the system just as the civil war started so he fought in the war, for the Union. He served under General Wynston Jamison Panton, who apparently took young Charles under his wing and even saved his life during one of the final battles. Panton housed Charles while he recovered from his wounds after the war. After that, Charles worked as a butler for the General for many years."

Noticing that Lena was tiring, Gwyn moved the tray of food and helped prop Lena's head comfortably with pillows. "After Queenie Panton died, the General retrieved his daughters, who had been living with her on the east coast because she had some heart problems and had been unable to live at Glen Eyrie for several years. The maid, Mitilde, was a good friend and comfort to the General. They became close, and Mitilde apparently became pregnant with the General's child. Naturally, Panton's stature in the community and many business dealings would have been threatened by knowledge of an interracial relationship. To complicate the situation, the Ku Klux Klan was running rampant in Colorado at the time and had much of the state's political dealings in its grasp."

Gwyn raised a finger in the air before continuing. "So, get this! Charles – who felt he owed the General a debt of gratitude for saving his life and keeping him employed all those years – accepted a bizarre offer from the General. The agreement was that Charles would marry Mitilde and return to Charles' home state of Georgia, raising the child as his own. In return, the General would provide property and ample funds for Charles, Mitilde, and the baby to live in comfort. The final part of the deal was that the General could visit and would be referred to by the couple as Charles' wartime buddy and close family friend."

Lena's sluggish brain slowly processed what Gwyn had said. "So basically, the General was protecting Mitilde and the unborn baby from the KKK while simultaneously protecting himself from becoming a social outcast through this arrangement, right?" Gwyn nodded affirmatively.

"Lena, the letter is a handwritten agreement between the two men, and there is something about it that I think we had best look into as soon as possible," Gwyn said. She stopped speaking and put on a forced smile as Kacie strode casually through the doorway.

"Hey, Lena. You look a little better!" Kacie exclaimed as she perched herself on the side of Lena's hospital bed. "I brought you one of Gwyn's chocolate croissants in case you decide to eat and want something other than hospital food. Oh, and Jasmyn called. She asked me to tell you that the assessor's valuation of the Glen Eyrie estate came in at $41,649,000. Ain't that a pretty chunk of change?!" Lena smiled weakly and nodded.

Kacie and Gwyn planned to explore the area behind the rear wall of the closet in the maid's garret after dinner. If Lena was awake, they hoped to include her and Jasmyn in the exploration via Facetime. Lena was worried about the safety of Gwyn and Kacie exploring alone, so Gwyn agreed to call Calvin to see if he would be willing to accompany them.

Barbie entered the room and, pleased to see that Lena had eaten a small amount, announced that Lena would be transferred to a regular room within the hour. Gwyn handed Barbie Lena's travel bag and asked her to ensure that someone gave Lena her cell phone once she was out of the intensive care unit. Gwyn put on her coat and gloves before kissing her sister on the cheek and heading out into the bone-chilling Colorado snow.

Chapter Eight Recipes

Easy Chocolate croissants

> 1 tube Pillsbury ® Original Crescent Rolls
> Milk chocolate chips
> Penzey's Vanilla Sugar
> 1 egg white

Directions:

1. Preheat oven to 375 degrees.

2. Place parchment paper on a cookie sheet (or grease pan)

3. Separate dough into triangles.

4. Place 2 T. chocolate chips on the longest edge of each triangle.

5. Roll each triangle loosely from the longest edge to the furthest point.

6. Pinch open areas together.

7. Brush each croissant with egg whites and sprinkle with Penzey's Vanilla Sugar.

8. Bake until golden brown (11 – 13 minutes).

— CHAPTER 9 —

The Safe Room

"Lawd, it's colder than a witch's titty in a brass bra in here!" Lena's new nurse exclaimed in a heavy southern drawl, winking at Lena as she fiddled with the thermostat. Tammy was a plump woman in her 30s with hair almost as big as her personality, blue eyeshadow, bright pink lipstick, and fake eyelashes.

Lena chuckled, grateful for the humor and the extra blanket Tammy placed over her. Her new room on the fourth floor of the hospital offered a window and more privacy than the ICU. Unlike the intensive care unit, Lena was permitted to use her computer and her cell phone, which Gwyn had left for her.

Dr. Winslow came by to check her feet and was not surprised to learn that Lena was struggling with pain between medication doses. "The good news is you get to keep your toes, but I'm afraid I have some sobering news. Today and tonight will likely be the worst in terms of the pain in your feet, Lena."

The handsome doctor sat on the side of her bed. "Stitches on the bottom of your feet are at high risk for infection and take time to heal. If you walk with stitches in your feet, you will be in sorry shape. So, in order to prevent infection and the possibility of putting too much pressure on your stitches, you will be in a wheelchair for a few days with very minimal weight bearing. Since you will be taking medication for pain, you absolutely must not drive for at least a week, and you will need to work with physical therapy daily. When you are ready, we will transition you from a wheelchair to a walker, probably for 2 – 3 days, and then to crutches until your feet are healed well enough to bear your full weight."

Personal freedom had always been important to Lena. Being single and independent meant she could travel and live as she pleased; thus, functioning as a single invalid was a circumstance Lena could not fathom. Worried about how she would take care of herself, where she could stay, and how she would get home, Lena placed a worried hand on her forehead. "I am single, and I do not think my sister can be with me 24 hours a day for that long. I don't know what to do" she said as her eyes filled with tears.

"For tonight, let us focus on getting your pain under control" the doctor said. "We have an inpatient rehabilitation unit here at the hospital. When you are discharged – which would be Wednesday at the absolute soonest, I recommend we transfer you there for a few days, Lena." Dr. Winslow smiled and paused. "That will give you time to figure out next steps, and I can have my good friend and colleague, Dr. Monte Jarrett, oversee your care there. As for being single… well, I cannot imagine why. I am sure you have broken a few hearts along the way."

Lena nodded and wiped a stray tear from her cheek. "Thank you. I would appreciate that. This has all been pretty overwhelming." Dr. Winslow nodded and smiled, and Lena noticed with amusement that her heartbeat quickened. She glanced at Dr. Winslow's left hand, pleased to see that he was not wearing a wedding ring.

"By the way," he said. "I understand my dad is accompanying your sister and friend this evening. Something about a hidden room at Glen Eyrie?"

Lena sighed heavily. "Your father seems to be a wonderful man. Given what happened to me, I am really grateful Calvin will be with them. I am scared someone else is going to get hurt." The doctor's expression changed to one of concern as he held her gaze for an instant, but before he could ask for clarification the medicine cart arrived. He discussed a change in Lena's pain medication with Tammy, then encouraged Lena to rest and left so the nurse could draw Lena's blood and administer her medications.

The pain medication brought both relief and drowsiness. As her head swam and her eyelids became heavy, Lena saw the maid sitting at the end of her bed, smiling peacefully. *Rest, child. I will watch over you.* Intellectually Lena knew that the appropriate reaction to the maid ought to be fear, but instead she felt comforted and safe as she surrendered to the potent medication and fell into a tranquil slumber.

An incoming text message from Kacie awakened Lena shortly after 7:30 that evening.

> Hey! We're ready to see what's behind the closet in the garret. Calvin is here with us. Are you up for joining us? If so, Gwyn will Facetime you (I'll Facetime Jasmyn).

> Just woke up – yes, I can Facetime. Glad Calvin is with you.

> Cool! We will call in just a minute.

When the Facetime call came in Lena could not help but laugh at the sight of her younger sister. Gwyn was sporting an elastic band with a headlamp around her head. Calvin and Kacie were wearing headlamps, too. They had placed several covered lanterns on the floor inside the maid's room, casting a soft glow across the room. Calvin had brought the knight up through the elevator and placed it at the bottom of the ladder against the peculiar half door to keep it open. Focused on the safety of her sister and dearest friend, Lena wondered whether moving the knight from the salt circle Dillon had placed around it would present problems.

Lena watched from the darkness of her hospital room as Calvin ascended the narrow stone staircase, sweeping away cobwebs with a broom held above his head. Gwyn followed behind carrying a large flashlight and her cell phone which enabled Lena to see to the extent that the low light and her small cell phone screen would permit. Kacie carried a lantern and followed Gwyn.

When Calvin reached the landing he exclaimed, "Well I'll be! I think this might be a safe room!" At the top of the landing was a small room with a bed, dressing table and chair, and a wash basin.

"What is a safe room?" Kacie asked as she reached the landing.

"In my American History class, we learned about safe rooms. They were used as part of the Underground Railroad prior to and during the Civil War to hide and protect slaves," Jasmyn offered through Kacie's phone. "But the castle was built after the war ended. Wonder why they thought they needed a safe room?"

Calvin suggested that General Panton was known as a civil rights leader, and that as such he may have built the room in case the maid or his own family ever needed to escape from the KKK. In fact, Calvin shared he had read that Panton had made very generous donations to Hampton University in Virginia, which was built after the end of the Civil War specifically for educating freed Black citizens, and there was a building on the campus named in his honor.

Calvin was in mid-sentence when Gwyn's flashlight died, and a silvery orb of light appeared that grew as it hovered near the dressing table. Kacie and Gwyn were unaware that their cell phone batteries had drained completely, disconnecting Jasmyn and Lena from the video calls. Gwyn, Calvin, and Kacie stood motionless as the orb grew and its softly glowing shape shifted into that of a person.

Within seconds, standing before them was a tall middle-aged White man in a brown pinstriped suit and vest. His wavy brown hair was parted neatly on the side, and he wore a moustache that curled upwards at the ends. The spirit bowed his head slightly, smiled directly at Gwyn, and pointed at the dressing table before disappearing. A man's voice filled the room. *The letters are in the dressing table.*

Ten minutes after the video call dropped, Lena received a text from Gwyn.

Cell phones and flashlights died – we are fine. Did you see the ghost? He led us to the dressing table where we found bundles of letters from Mitilde to the General! Will bring them with me to show you tomorrow.

Glad you are safe! No, I didn't see anything unusual on my end. Can't wait to see the letters. Hey - earlier you said there was something important you wanted to tell me about the agreement from the butler's trunk?

Let's talk in the morning. BTW, I heard back from Uncle Billy. Will forward you his e-mail in the morning – you really must see it to believe it. Love you! There by 9:30 tomorrow, weather permitting. Snow is awful. Please rest - and keep trying to eat.

A nurse awakened Lena in the morning with a breakfast menu and her scheduled medications. The pain in her feet was, as Dr. Winslow had suggested it would be, less intense than it had been the prior evening. Lena enjoyed a bowl of toasted oat cereal, a cup of coffee and some strawberry yogurt before the pain medication required yet another nap from her.

She dreamt vividly of Mitilde and the General, who were outside on a warm sunny day with a slender, balding Caucasian man. They were seated on the porch of a small, narrow house laughing and drinking lemonade while two little girls played with dolls on a blanket in the shade of a large tree. The light-skinned Black girls appeared to be twins, and it looked as though they were having a tea party with their dolls.

The handmade dolls appeared to have been made from black socks and had embroidered facial features with black beads for eyes. Each doll had curly black yarn hair and wore a white cotton petticoat over cotton floral dresses, one of which was yellow and the other blue. One of the girls skipped happily from the blanket to Wynston Panton and asked, "Papa Panton, please will you come play dollies with us?"

My babies. A cool breeze and the sound of Mitilde's voice woke Lena up from her nap. Though Lena could not see the maid, the cool temperature of the room made Lena suspicious that the breeze and the voice might not have been part of her dream. Lena was struck by the realization that she rarely recalled vivid details from dreams, but that on the occasions she had dreamt about the maid she was able to recall distinct colors, smells, words, and sounds.

An orderly arrived and provided her with a sponge bath, which helped Lena feel more alert. After helping Lena get comfortable on clean sheets and showing her how to use the large plastic remote to control the bed position, lights, and television, the orderly left. Lena was absently watching local news coverage of the winter storm when Gwyn arrived carrying a paper bag and a cardboard drink carrier from The Perk Downtown coffee shop.

"Jade citrus mint tea with honey for your throat," Gwyn said as she set her things down on the broad window ledge. She handed a warm cup to Lena and kissed her forehead. After taking off her winter coat, scarf and gloves, Gwyn perched herself on the side of Lena's bed and briefly studied her sister's face. "You look a million times better this morning, Lena. How do you feel?"

"Quite a bit better," Lena said, savoring a sip of the warm tea. "Thank you for this. Will you please hand me my lotion and deodorant from my bag? Then I want to hear all about last night – I was unable to see much on my phone."

Thankful to see Lena more clear-headed, Gwyn retrieved Lena's bag. She replied that the past 48 hours had been eventful, and for Lena to fully understand Gwyn needed to share the events of the past two days chronologically. "Do you remember what I shared with you yesterday?"

"Yes, but my head was a bit foggy. As I recall, Charles the butler agreed to marry Mitilde the maid, who was pregnant by General Panton. Charles agreed to it out of a sense of obligation because the general cared for him after he was injured on the battlefield, and then employed him as a butler. In exchange, General Panton agreed to make sure Charles and Mitilde had enough money to live comfortably. Did I get everything right?"

Gwyn nodded. "Yes, you did. I'm surprised you remember anything at all – you were pretty loopy when we spoke. I brought Charles' journal for you to read when you feel up to it. The journal only spans one month, but it is an interesting read once you get used to his handwriting." Gwyn set the old leather journal on the hospital table tray over Lena's lap.

"The other thing that was in the trunk with Charles' journal was this," Gwyn said as she removed a yellowed envelope from the paper bag. The envelope had been sealed with old-fashioned red sealing wax, which bore a "WJP" embossed monogram. Written on the front of the envelope in jagged writing was "To be opened only in the event of questions pertaining to the Panton estate." Lena ran her fingers over the wax seal, then gently removed a rough-edged, handwritten document from the envelope.

On this 6th day of June in the year of our Lord 1895, Mr. Charles A. Fuller and Gen'l Wynston J. Panton hereby enter into this binding agreement, which shall be kept in secrecy for our respective lifetimes unless mutually agreed.

Whereas Ms. Mitilde Freeman is with child conceived through amorous congress with Mr. Panton, and whereas interracial congress may result in violence toward Ms. Freeman and the unborn, and whereas Mr. Panton maintains familial and political and business interests which must be protected, and whereas Mr. Fuller is a widower without children and is indebted to Mr. Panton for rescue from life-threatening war injury, therefore Mr. Fuller shall wed Ms. Freeman On the 7th day of June in the year of our Lord, 1895.

Mr. Fuller shall be dutiful in his responsibilities as husband to Ms. Freeman and father to the unborn child. In return Mr. Panton shall provide a modest home and property for farming in Mr. Fuller's town of origin, Cordele, Georgia, and sufficient annual salary to enable the Fuller family to exist in comfort as may be practical for the family.

Regular visitation to the Fuller family shall be afforded Mr. Panton. The Fullers shall reference Mr. Panton in truth as Mr. Fuller's dear friend and battle colleague.

The aforementioned enter into this agreement in gratitude and secrecy for the protection of all parties. Signed on the 6th day of June in the year of our Lord 1895.

Mr. Charles Abraham Fuller   Mr. Wynston Jamison Panton

Lena stared at the document as she processed its contents. "Cordele? That's a coincidence" Lena mused. Gwyn nodded. Lena told Gwyn about her dream earlier that morning and wondered aloud whether the twin girls in the dream were a true revelation or just a strange dream influenced by her medications or the stress she had experienced in the most recent couple of days.

Gwyn's eyes widened in disbelief. "This is unbelievable, Lena. I have the answer. The answer is yes, Mitilde was carrying twins. Now, if you are up for it, I have one more thing I need you to read." Lena nodded as Gwyn pulled Lena's laptop out of its case and set it on the wheeled hospital tray over Lena's lap.

"Log in and open your e-mail" Gwyn said. "There is a long, and somewhat complicated e-mail from Uncle Billy that you need to understand. Do you want to read it on your own, or do you want me to read it to you?" Feeling relatively clear-headed, Lena decided to read it on her own.

Dear Gwyn,

Retirement is great in the summer months when I can golf and we can travel to the beach, but this winter your Aunt Becky and I have been digging into our respective family histories. I have been mentoring a junior senator, as well – it keeps me sharp and in the know, but I sure don't miss being a state senator!

I was planning on writing up what I've learned about my side of the family and assembling the photos I gathered as a Christmas gift for you and Lena, but I'm happy to give you a sneak peek. So glad you asked! Most of this I learned from ancestry.com, my grandmother Mitilde's diary, old family stories, and a typewritten family history document I found in a box with my mother's will after she passed on.

My grandmother Mitilde's father (my great grandfather) was named Absolom. Family stories say that he and his wife Awah were slaves on a cotton plantation outside of Savannah. They were apparently freed when Sherman's army burnt the plantation and freed the slaves (according to history, Sherman stormed Savannah in late December 1864). Absolom and Awah adopted the last name Freeman, as many freed slaves did.

Absolom was befriended by an abolitionist who helped Awah, who was pregnant, and their son Samuel find a temporary home with a sympathetic white couple in Macon. Sherman's March appealed to Absolom, so he apparently stayed in Georgia after Sherman's departure and continued to fight for the Union. He was killed April 16, 1865 in the Battle of Columbus on the Alabama-Georgia border. He is buried at Andersonville National Cemetery – I was up in Andersonville for a meeting last October and saw Absolom's grave for myself.

Awah gave birth to Mitilde Salena Thomas in May of 1865. Several years later Awah and the two children apparently found their way north. Awah worked as a domestic servant for a wealthy family, the Pantons, in Beaufort, South Carolina. During the election protests in 1870, Samuel was beaten and killed by the Ku Klux Klan. Sad, isn't it, that Awah lost both her husband and her son? Anyway, Awah's employer relocated to Delaware in 1871, and it appears that Awah and Mitilde moved to Delaware with them.

There is no formal record of what happened to Awah, but I remember mama saying Awah died from Tuberculosis. At some point her daugh-

ter Mitilde went to work as a housemaid for one of the Pantons' sons out west. The son's name was Wynston, and he was a Civil War hero (Union) who made a lot of money in railroading. Mitilde married Panton's butler, a white man named Charles Thomas, in Colorado Springs on June 7, 1895 (he was 51 and she was 29 when they married). They must have moved to Cordele shortly after that.

In July 1895 Mr. Panton purchased a 4-acre parcel of land from a James O. Farnell here in Cordele. I am not sure whether the shotgun house was on the land or if it was built afterwards, but I remember that place. Anyway, Panton signed the deed to the land over to Charles in September 1895. Charles and Mitilde's twin daughters Marie and Wilhelmina were born January 2, 1896 in Cordele. Wilhelmina was grandmother to me and your mom – she and your mom were particularly close.

Anyway, Charles and Mitilde grew peanuts on the land. They sold peanuts to the railroad station, which was about a mile from the farm, and Mitilde provided laundry service for railroad workers for quite a few years. In 1902 Panton came to Cordele and stayed for nearly a year. I know that because local newspapers document that while he was here, he built the general store in town. Records show that Panton signed the deed for the general store over to Charles in 1903. I don't know why Panton was so generous to Charles and Mitilde, but what a guy!

Charles died in 1914 (cause of death is listed on his death certificate as Bright's disease), and Mitilde never remarried. Their daughter Marie married a white man named Wesley Walker in 1915, and Wilhelmina married my grandpa Thurston Davenport (of course, he was white, as you know) in 1916. Mitilde was 61 when she passed in her sleep on March 28, 1926. After that Marie and her husband took over the general store, and it is still run by distant cousins today, though it can't be generating much profit with all the new modern places and chains that have moved into Cordele in the past ten years or so.

Wilhelmina ("Willi") and Thurston were my grandparents, and they lived on the land on 8th Street for many years (records show the city repossessed it in 1955 due to years of unpaid property tax). The old parcel of land is now part of a watermelon farm, but the remnants of the old shotgun house are still there. It has been 15 years or so since you and Lena and I went in there. The roof is partially collapsed now, but the front is still standing, and it is no longer visible from the road because of all the trees.

Willi and Thurston had a daughter (your Granny M, who was my mother) who was born in 1922. Thurston and Willi named the baby Matilde after Wilhelmina's mother. Just so you know, they also had two sons. The first, Charles Alan (my uncle) died of heart failure in the early 1950s. The second son was stillborn. Granddad Thurston died of a stroke in 1964 and Grandma Willi passed in 1966 from pneumonia.

My mother (your Granny M) - married my father, William Winthrop Thomas (your Papa Willie), in 1942. Your aunt Eleanor was born in 1944. You probably don't remember her because she died in a car accident in 1989 when you were about 5 years old, Gwyn, but it is possible that Lena might remember her since she is four years older. I was born in 1947, and your mom, Flora Jo, was born in 1949.

You can't tell by looking at my generation or yours that we have black ancestors, Gwyn, but this is an important part of our heritage. I often wonder how Charles and Mitilde were treated as an interracial couple back in the day – Lord knows racism is still prevalent and ugly in Cordele even today. I hope this answers your questions - am thrilled that you asked. I'm meeting my mentee for lunch in an hour, so I've got to shave and get dressed.

Love,
Uncle Billy

Disbelief swept over Lena. While her mind was incapable of following the lineage in the moment, she understood clearly that if the content of Uncle Billy's e-mail was accurate then she and Gwyn might be descendants of Wynston Jamison Panton. If so, Lena wondered whether that might explain the reason Mitilde's spirit had referred to Lena as *my child* the previous evening. Lena covered her face with her hands and squeezed her eyes shut, trying desperately to comprehend Uncle Billy's letter.

Gwyn gently pulled Lena's hands away from her face. "I had to draw it out to wrap my head around it, Lena." Gwyn said as she opened a spiral notebook and handed it to Lena. "I diagramed the family tree as Uncle Billy described it. The bottom line, Lena, is that I think you and I might be the great-great granddaughters of General Panton!" Lena studied the diagram Gwyn had drawn.

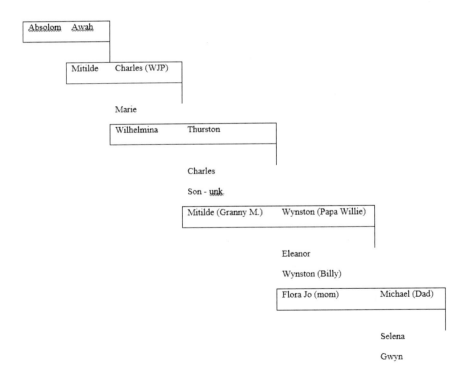

Lena closed her eyes, laid her head back on her pillows, and again covered her face with her hands. Gwyn looked at her older sister with concern. Lena had always been the stronger and wiser of the two sisters as far as Gwyn was concerned, but Gwyn had not considered whether sharing what she had discovered with Lena might be overwhelming given her condition and the events of the most recent few days. "Oh, sis. I am so sorry. This is all too much for you right now. Really, I should have known better."

"No, Gwyn. I am fine." Lena uncovered her face and shrugged her shoulders. "It is just a lot to take in and the medication they have me on makes my brain painfully slow. What concerns me the most right now is several relationships that matter to me. David and Ben have become friends of mine. I treasure their friendship, and Ria is incredibly special to them."

Lena winced from a twinge of pain in her right foot before continuing. "I agreed to come to Colorado Springs to take a look at Glen Eyrie, have it appraised, and advise Ria about whether selling the estate would be in her best interest. I agreed to do this as a personal favor to David and Ben. This could get complicated, and it could impact my friendship with David and Ben. Even if you are correct about us being descendants of General Panton, Gwyn, I do not think that pursuing any portion of the estate is something we should do."

"Oh, wow – I hadn't even considered the idea that the estate might be in play. Well, we do not have to figure anything out today, and it looks like your lunch is here" Gwyn said gently as an orderly arrived with a tray of food. "Why don't you eat something and get some shut eye? Kacie and I need to tell you about the room behind the closet and what we found last night, so we will come back together this evening if the roads are not too bad. She needs to head back to Denver tomorrow morning, you know. All those athletes need her TLC."

Gwyn left Charles' journal on the tray table for Lena to read. "By the way, that grilled cheese looks awful. I promise to bring you something decent for dinner later if the roads are passable. I love you, Lena bean!" Gwyn donned her coat, scarf, and gloves, then pulled an extra blanket from the closet and placed it over Lena's lap.

Uninterested in eating and unable to sleep, Lena watched the television for a while and then decided to read Charles' journal. Charles wrote at length of his fondness and respect for the general and wrote with certainty that he would have died from his injuries had General Panton not rescued him and carried him to safety by horseback during one of the final battles of the Civil War. He had requested to work for General Panton in some capacity as soon as his injuries were sufficiently healed.

The butler wrote that he had agonized for many years over leaving his younger sister behind at the orphanage, but they had exchanged letters faithfully. For Charles, the move to Georgia offered an opportunity to reconnect with his sister, who was married with children and living in Atlanta. He wrote of his pending marriage to Mitilde as a form of repayment to the general, whom he repeatedly referred to as the only friend he had known since leaving the orphanage to fight in the 'war between the states'.

He had been married briefly to a young schoolteacher who perished from scarlet fever within weeks of their nuptials. Charles wrote that he and Mitilde would provide companionship for one another and parenting for the baby she carried, which he would raise as his own. They would live in Cordele, home to the orphanage in which Charles and his sister had been raised. Cordele, Georgia was, he wrote, the only home he had ever known.

When Kacie and Gwyn arrived that evening, the doctor on duty had already been in to check Lena's feet and her bandages had been changed. She had just been given her evening pain medication and was reading Charles' final journal entry while tears streamed down her face.

"That poor man!" she said softly as Kacie and Gwyn removed their coats. "Charles never knew parents' love. His wife died. He never had children of his own. His employer was the closest thing he had to a friend. The whole thing is just so incredibly sad and tragic!"

"I had the same reaction," Gwyn said. "But I would like to think that maybe he and Mitilde eventually fell in love, or at least became close domestic partners." Gwyn opened a large plastic food storage container while Kacie set out three sturdy paper plates.

"I made you your favorite!" Gwyn said proudly.

"You made chicken and chaffle bombs?" Lena asked excitedly. Gwyn nodded and placed a homemade waffle topped with bacon and fried chicken on each plate, then drizzled it with the bourbon cayenne maple syrup that Lena adored.

"You are the best sister ever, Gwyndolyn Thomas!" For the first time since Saturday evening, Lena ate a full meal. She was licking the last bit of syrup from her fork when someone knocked on the door.

"Delivery for Miss Lena Thomas" said a freckle-faced young man holding a glossy Tiffany blue box tied with a large silver satin bow.

"That's me," Lena said. The boy entered the room and handed the box to Lena. Gwyn handed the young man a five-dollar bill and reminded him to drive carefully on the icy roads. Lena removed the small red envelope tucked under the ribbon and pulled out a card, which read, *I am not working today, so thought I'd send you something to keep you company and something to keep you occupied. Will Winslow*

Lena bit her bottom lip in a failed attempt to keep the smile from her face, but Kacie grabbed the card and read it aloud. Lena blushed and gave her sister a mischievous grin. Gwyn moved Lena's dinner plate so she could open the box. Lena untied the silver ribbon and lifted the top of the box; inside was a plush teddy bear dressed in a mint green hospital gown and the latest issue of *Colorado Homes & Lifestyles* magazine.

"Well, my friend, it looks like you have caught the good doctor's attention, Lena Thomas!" Kacie winked and giggled. "And my goodness, the man made a mighty strong first move!"

Kacie walked to the window and assessed the weather. "Lena, it is snowing pretty hard, and this storm is expected to pack a punch. I have to be back at work tomorrow, so I've got to hit the road. Please, sweet friend, take care of yourself." Kacie planted a kiss on Lena's cheek and promised to return over the weekend.

As Kacie zipped her ivory down puffy coat, Lena teasingly suggested that Kacie resembled the giant puffy marshmallow character from the Ghostbuster movie.

"Hey, you twerp! I think you need to share some of those pain meds with me!" Kacie stuck her tongue out at Lena as she exited the room, middle finger of her right hand extended into the air. Gwyn thought Lena's comment about Kacie resembling the Jet Puff Marshmallow man was hilarious and enjoyed a hearty laugh.

When she regained her composure, Gwyn assured Lena that she would be enjoying – and taking good care of – Lena's Land Rover so Kacie could drive Gwyn's car back to Denver. Gwyn tidied up the dinner plates and rinsed the plastic containers in the bathroom sink, then packed the food containers and silverware into a large reusable canvas grocery bag. Fidgeting with her fingers, Gwyn seemed to be procrastinating putting on her coat.

A puzzled look from Lena prompted a deep sigh from Gwyn, who gave her sister a serious look. "Lena, I have taken the rest of the week off work, but I have to be honest about something. I am just too afraid to stay in the castle overnight by myself. Do you think I could use your credit card to get a hotel room?"

"That won't be necessary," said a woman's voice from the doorway. "You can stay with me at the carriage house as long as you would like." It was Ria, carrying a tall vase of blush roses and stargazer lilies with eucalyptus. She set the flowers on Lena's hospital tray and squeezed Lena's hand. Then she extended her hand to Gwyn and introduced herself.

"Warning, incoming kid-nado!" bellowed a man's voice from the doorway. It was Ben, who had his two sons in tow. One boy was carrying a mylar balloon that read, *Get Well Soon,* and the other boy was carrying a Los Angeles International Airport shopping bag. Ben strode casually to Lena's bedside and planted a kiss on her forehead. "Damn, Lena," he said, looking at her with concern. "Your aura is dull, darling. We should never have involved you in this. I'm really sorry this happened to you."

"This was no one's fault, Ben." Lena said. Ben took the airport shopping bag from his youngest son and pulled out a chocolate brown faux fur blanket. It was the perfect gift for Lena, who was chilly, slightly dizzy, and increasingly tired. With a knowing glance at the two young boys, who were deeply engaged in a thumb war, Ria moved the vase of flowers to the windowsill and introduced Ben to Gwyn.

Ben shook Gwyn's hand and told her that David had insisted they return to Colorado Springs when he heard that Lena was hospitalized. David would return to Colorado in a few days after his tour wrapped up. Ria look worried, and assured Gwyn that she would cover any expenses related to Lena's incident.

"Oh, Lena" Ria said as she sat on the edge of the bed and reached for Lena's hand. "The castle has always been haunted, like I told you. But the ghosts have never hurt anyone before. I am so sorry this happened to you!" Lena assured Ria that the situation was simply a highly unusual sleepwalking incident, and not anything the castle spirits had intentionally done. Ria responded, but Lena was too tired to understand what Ria said. The level of her eyelids was increasingly disproportionate to the level of food in her stomach, and the pain medications were adding to her inability to stay awake.

Noticing that Lena was having difficulty keeping her eyes open, Ben motioned to Ria. He covered Lena with the faux fur blanket and the boys enjoyed helping him gently tuck it in around her. Ria insisted that Gwyn stay in the carriage house with her for as long as she needed. Besides, Ria said, Ben and the boys would be leaving in a day or two once the roads cleared up.

Ben, Ria, and the boys donned their winter coats and gloves and exited the hospital room quietly. Lena was already asleep, so Gwyn decided she would have to wait until Wednesday to tell Lena about the safe room behind the closet in Mitilde's room. Before Gwyn left, she placed a reusable grocery bag in the closet next to Lena's overnight bag.

Gwyn draped her coat and scarf over her left arm, then bent down to kiss her sister's cheek before leaving. She noted with concern that Lena was feverish, and her face had paled. Gwyn stopped by the nurse's station to let the nurses know she thought Lena might have a fever. She hesitated before putting on her winter gear and heading out into the brisk Colorado blizzard, then decided that staying at the carriage house with Ria would be the wisest decision.

Chapter Nine Recipes

Chicken 'n Chaffle bombs

Chaffles (savory cheddar waffles – makes 4)

> Two eggs
> 3/4 c. shredded cheddar cheese
> ¼ c. shredded Parmesan cheese
> 1 t. Penzey's Tuscan Sunset seasoning
> 1 T. almond flour
> 1 t. garlic salt

Directions:

1. Preheat mini waffle iron
2. In a mixing bowl, combine all ingredients and mix well.
3. Spritz waffle iron with cooking spray and carefully pour ¼ c chaffle batter into waffle iron.
4. Cook 3 – 4 minutes or until waffle begins to brown.

Chicken:

> 2 chicken breasts cut in half and pounded to an even thickness
> Vegetable oil (for frying)
> 1 c. buttermilk
> 1 c. flour
> ½ c. cornstarch
> 2 T. pureed chipotle in adobo
> 1 T. white sugar
> 1 t. garlic powder
> 1/8 t. cinnamon
> 1 t. smoked paprika
> 1 t. salt
> 1 t. pepper
> 1 t. cayenne pepper

Directions:

1. Combine buttermilk and pureed chipotle in adobo in a small bowl with a whisk.

2. Place chicken in the buttermilk mixture.

3. Combine dry ingredients in a bowl and mix well.

4. Dredge each piece of chicken in the flour mixture, ensuring an even coat.

5. Fry chicken in oil one inch deep until golden brown and cooked through.

6. Allow chicken to rest on paper towels to absorb excess oil.

Bacon:

8 slices bacon chopped, fried, and spooned onto paper towel lined plate to absorb excess grease.

Cayenne Bourbon Maple Syrup

¼ c. inexpensive bourbon

1 c. maple syrup

1 t. cayenne pepper

2 T. margarine

Directions:

1. Combine syrup, cayenne pepper and bourbon in a small saucepan over medium-high heat and simmer, whisking frequently, for 4 – 6 minutes until liquid reduces.

2. Remove pan from heat, whisk in margarine.

Plating:

1. Place a chaffle on each plate and top with a piece of fried chicken.

2. Sprinkle bacon bits over the chicken.

3. Drizzle with syrup or serve with syrup in a dipping bowl.

— CHAPTER 10 —

Mitilde's Letters

Wednesday's dull morning light peeked through the closed curtains in Lena's hospital room. Although the pain in her feet had improved, a low-grade fever and nausea had returned, and according to her nurse, Lena's pulse was slightly elevated. Lena raised the head of her bed and concentrated on the ceiling tiles, trying to wish the nausea away.

"Hard to tell from up here, but we got about 18 inches of snow last night, with at least another 12 inches expected today," the nurse told her. She opened the curtains so Lena could see the snow, then left to consult with the doctor on duty while Lena drifted in and out of a sickening, nauseated sleep.

"You know, Ms. Thomas, you were supposed to be transferred to the inpatient rehab unit today." Dr. Winslow said quietly. Lena opened her eyes to see the handsome, green-eyed doctor seated in a chair next to her bed. She smiled slightly. "Sepsis is a serious illness, and it can be difficult to treat. I have ordered Piperacillin as an addition to your course of antibiotics, and we will get you intravenous medication and a new patch for nausea. We'll also start to decrease the pain medication, but we need to keep you here for at least another 24 hours to make sure the infection is under control."

Lena nodded and used the bed remote to raise herself to a near sitting position. "Not feeling too great today, honestly." She met his sea green eyes and, for just an instant, thought she might not be able to escape them. "Thank you for the gift. It brightened my day yesterday."

"Lena, you were doing so well that I was certain you would be transferred to inpatient rehab today. Once you are transferred, you will no longer be my patient. Professionally that will be rewarding because it means you are recovering." His eyes again locked with hers, and she could not bring herself to look away. "Personally, though, I am looking forward to your transfer because once you are no longer my patient, I would like to get to know you on a personal level. That is, if you'd have any interest?"

Still locked into his gaze, Lena replied "I would like that very much. Besides, if you have any interest at all given what I must look like in this hospital bed, then I know you are *at least* as crazy as I am."

The doctor threw his head back and laughed. "I *can* be crazy. But if this is your worst, I cannot wait to see you when you are at your best. How about we start by agreeing that you will call me Will?"

"Fine, as long as you agree to call me Lena and do something about this awful nausea. It would be awful to vomit in front of you." Lena closed her eyes and absently rubbed the back of her neck with her right hand.

Will nodded and smiled. "It's a deal. And please don't worry, I see people vomit all the time. It might not be your best look, but I do not think it would be a deal breaker. Looks like your neck is bothering you, so I will have the nurse bring you a warm neck wrap and will also make arrangements to have physical therapy come by later today. They can teach you some stretches you can do while you are stuck in bed. In the meantime, would it be okay with you if I call your sister and give her an update on your condition? I understand she was quite worried when she left last night."

Lena nodded, realizing that she could not remember Gwyn, Ria, Ben, or the boys leaving the previous evening. The last thing she remembered was being tucked in by the boys, who had laughed and told her she looked like a giant brown hairy hot dog. Will assured her that small lapses in memory were perfectly normal given her situation, then he left to continue his morning rounds after promising to check back in on her later in the day.

The medicine cart arrived shortly after Will left, and Lena was grateful that the IV medication brought almost instant relief from the nausea. The nurse applied a new patch behind her ear and brought a warm neck wrap and a cool washcloth for Lena's forehead. Lena had half of a piece of dry toast, some ice chips, and a few sips of ginger ale for breakfast. She was so cold that her teeth chattered, but she did not have the energy to pull up the faux fur blanket Ben had brought for her. Lena closed her eyes and waited for the chills to pass.

Rest, my child. Mitilde's voice said. Lena opened her eyes slightly and watched as the maid materialized. Mitilde became as solid as a real person and pulled the blanket up over Lena's shivering body. *I am sorry about your feet. Please forgive me.*

"I forgive you, Mitilde" Lena whispered. "Please keep my sister safe."

I will. Mitilde stood next to Lena's bed with her hands folded in front of her, fingers interlaced. Lena noticed that the maid's eyes were the same as her own mother's eyes. They were the color of onyx and her penetrating stare seemed to reflect a deep sorrow and longing. Lena struggled against a long, drowsy blink. When she opened her eyes Mitilde was gone.

For several minutes Lena watched heavy, wet snowflakes fall lazily outside the window of her hospital room. She pulled the blanket up over her cold nose and ears and nestled into its soft warmth. As she drifted to sleep Lena thought she could smell Charlie perfume, a scent her mother had often worn. Lena dreamt vividly of a conversation with her mother in which she implored Lena to use her blessings to benefit others. "Change hearts and lives, my Lena. Be wise with your blessings."

Ding. The familiar, nagging sound of an incoming text wakened Lena abruptly. She ignored it and tried to return to the dream of her mother, but to no avail. A second *ding* was intrusive enough for Lena to open her eyes. She raised the head of her bed and reached for her phone. She opened the Notes app on her cell phone and typed *change hearts and lives wise blessings* just in case she forgot what she had dreamt. Lena sat up, pondering whether the dream had any real meaning, and then read the text message from Gwyn.

Lena, text me when you are awake and up for a chat. Dr. Winslow (aka Prince Charming) called – I know you're having a rough day. Roads are horrible, but we need to talk!
G

Just woke up – am pretty groggy. Call me in 15 minutes?

OK. BTW, when your nurse comes in have them bring you the canvas grocery bag I left in the closet with your overnight bag. Don't open it until we talk. Love you–

Feeling better than she had before her nap, Lena pressed the nurse call button on the corded remote that laid next to her. After helping Lena wash her face and brush her teeth the nurse checked her pulse and temperature, both of which showed improvement. The nurse made some notes, then went to get Lena some crackers, ice, and a ginger ale.

If I never see another cracker or can of ginger ale, that would be just fine with me, she thought. Lena was grumpy and weary of not feeling well. Being confined to a bed was in stark contrast to the active, busy lifestyle she normally enjoyed. Worse yet, the bottoms of her feet itched horribly. Lena sat up and gently rubbed the substantive gauze bandages on the bottom of her feet just enough to relieve the itching sensation. Taking a deep breath, she marveled at how much energy the simple act of sitting up seemed to consume.

Gwyn's video call was a welcome distraction from Lena's private pity party, which she spent several minutes sharing with her sister. Gwyn was wearing her winter coat and a scarf. She explained that the roads were impassable, but she needed to speak with Lena privately, so she was calling from Lena's car.

"Well," Gwyn said. "You are well enough to complain, so I'm going to consider that a blessing." Gwyn pulled her scarf up over her ears. "Lena, I want to tell you about the room behind the closet in Mitilde's room. Our cell phone batteries died, so you could not see what we saw, and I have not had a chance to tell you about it. Do you think you can focus on some details?"

Lena nodded and laid her head back on the pillows. Gwyn told her that at the top of the stairs was a small room. One wall of the room was a floor-to-ceiling built-in bookcase that held numerous old books on writing, mathematics, and nursing care. It was Kacie who had determined that Mitilde must have been studying to become a nurse.

Calvin believed that the room was a safe room in which the maid or the Panton family could hide if the KKK became a problem nearby, though Gwyn's suspicion was that in reality the room functioned as a place where Mitilde focused on her studies late at night. The room also contained a small bed, wash basin and a dressing table with a mirror. Because there was an old ink well on the dressing table, Gwyn believed it had been used as a desk. Gwyn then described the glowing ball of light and the apparition that had directed them to the letters in the drawer of the dressing table.

"Lena, there were bundles of letters in the drawer from Mitilde to General Panton." Gwyn paused to make sure Lena was comprehending everything before she continued. "Sis, listen carefully. General Panton bought Charles and Mitilde a small peanut farm in Cordele. Mitilde wasn't pregnant with one baby – she had twin girls, and she named them Marie and Wilhelmina."

"Wait a minute. Our great-grandma Willi had a twin sister named Marie" Lena said slowly, realizing the implications of what Gwyn was saying.

Gwyn nodded. "I am still reading through the letters, Lena, but I left four of them for you to read. They are in a canvas grocery bag with your personal belongings. Have the nurse get them out for you when you are up to doing some reading."

Lena agreed to read the letters, and then told Gwyn about her conversation with Will. After ending the video call, Lena texted Ria the assessor's valuation of the Glen Eyrie estate and called Kacie to make sure she had arrived home safely. Then she silenced her cell phone and took a nap.

She awoke in time for lunch. She ate half of a turkey sandwich and some gelatin. The nurse retrieved the grocery bag Gwyn had left in the closet next to Lena's overnight bag, and Lena settled in to read the four letters. The fragile letters were yellowed from age and smelled faintly of mildew. Lena traced the cursive script with her fingers, wondering whether it was really possible that she was related to the woman who had written the letters.

July 17, 1895

Dear Wynston:

> *The summer sun is more wicked the further east one travels, and the train cars were formidably hot. I am later than promised penning this letter because I was ill when we arrived in Atlanta.*

> *Charles' brother-in-law and sister own an inn near the train station. They permitted us to stay in a room in the back, but a white man and a black woman together is dangerous, especially in large towns. A doctor came, but I sensed he was unaccustomed to helping colored people. He thinks I am carrying two babies.*

> *We arrived in Cordele on Tuesday this week and were pleased that the construction of the house was complete. We stayed at Mr. and Mrs. Farnell's house in the servants' quarters until the furnishings and necessities for the house arrived Thursday afternoon. I never fancied I might have a house or such lovely belongings of my own! I am grateful, dear Wynston. Everything is far more than I could have imagined. At times I am guilt-ridden for having these things when many of my black brothers and sisters have so little.*

> *Your friend James Farnell is right nice. He has been overseeing the workers you hired to help Charles get the fields ready. The workers are not comfortable with a white man married to a black woman, but most of them just pay me no attention. Here I do not blend in with the black women because I am educated, and of course I should not attempt to get on with the white women.*

One of Mr. Farnell's workers has a wife named Sadie who is friendly. I will teach her to read and write, and she will teach me to grow vegetables and tend the chickens. Sadie says Mr. Farnell pays them well and lets them live in the old slave huts. Mr. Farnell is a kind person as you are, Wynston. He is helping many of my people, though we must not discuss the matter.

Charles will plant peanuts next week and we hope for good crops next spring. He is caring and keeps a watchful eye. Though he is aged to become a father, he will stand in for you admirably. Mr. Farnell's wife brought me a watermelon and some mint for the baby sickness, and Mr. Farnell sold Charles a gun for protection. We must take care with our safety, so I will keep the gun you provided in the house with me, and Charles will carry the new one with him.

Charles sends his best wishes. This fall he will make two cradles and I will sew quilts for two babies. Our babies, Wynston. This new life is frightening and exciting at once. I will be grateful always for your generosity, and I long for your company. Please write soon.

Sincerely,

Mitilde

September 5, 1895

Dear Wynston:

Thank you for your letter and for the lovely christening gowns. The baby sickness has finally subsided, but in its place, there is now an incessant hunger. I am certain I may not fit through the front door by the time the babies come.

I am concerned that you have not been feeling well, and hope that Evalynn, Flora, and Ruby are helping you. You need a maid to keep the castle up and prepare your meals – it is too much for your daughters, especially now that two of them are engaged to be married.

The peanuts are rooting well, and Mr. Farnell says we should have bountiful crops in the spring. I have taken a job doing laundry for some of the men who work at the railroad station and am enjoying my garden. The squash and pumpkin should be ready for harvesting in a month or so.

Charles says the town is planning for expansion to accommodate the railroad passengers. No one has come forward with funding or plans yet, but they say Cordele will grow as the railroad accommodates more travel. Mr. Farnell and Charles are negotiating with the rail station to provide peanuts and other goods to rail passengers starting next spring.

Last week Sadie's husband was injured by one of the Farnell's hogs that escaped from the pen. I was able to nurse him, and he will be fine after some time. Mrs. Farnell told the headmaster at the school that I went to nursing school so that he may call on me. I remain thankful to you and Queenie for investing in my education.

Charles and I have found comfort in one another's companionship. He is a decent man with good humor, and much more capable of farm work than I had dared hope. He helped with a local barn raising and seems to have made a friend. They go fishing on occasion, and they are working with a group of men to build a children's playground this winter.

I do miss our long talks, Wynston. Please attend to your health and write when you are able.

Sincerely,

Mitilde

January 8, 1896

Dear Wynston:

Our babies are here! Two girls, healthy and perfect. We named them Marie (after your Queenie) and Wilhelmina (after Mrs. Farnell, who has become a friend and confidante). Their skin is the most beautiful color, like that of a chestnut. Caring for two babies is exhausting. I never knew I could be so tired or so completely in love.

Wilhelmina (Willi) and Marie are my world, my whole heart. Sometimes I am sad that my mother is not here to guide me, but Sadie and Mrs. Farnell come by often and have taught me important things about mothering. I like to think mama would understand our arrangement and would be pleased that her granddaughters will grow up free.

Charles is quite enamored with the babies. He sings to them and talks to them as if they could understand his words. Charles and I are excited for you to meet them and look forward to your visit this May. Your last two letters brought us much joy. We adore the poems that you wrote for the babies, and we are both greatly relieved that your health has improved.

Over these past months my relationship with Charles has shifted from familiar companionship to deep friendship. I am beginning to feel love for him, though I am uncertain whether he feels similarly. Perhaps it is because of his tenderness with the twins or his care for me during pregnancy. You hoped and predicted this might happen. Perhaps you were right.

Sincerely,

Mitilde

July 13, 1896

Dear Wynston:

What a splendid blessing it was to have you visit for nearly a month. Mr. Wildman at the hotel said he never enjoyed a guest so much. The men are still talking about the barn raising you hosted here. In a state that still identifies with the Confederacy, whites and blacks volunteering together is uncommon. You have made quite an impression on the Cordele people.

The peanut crops look good, and the vegetables we planted last summer are yielding bountiful crops. Thank you again for the cows and pigs. The milk and meat will help Willi and Marie grow strong. It is becoming quite the menagerie here with the chickens, dogs, and barn cats! Recently a family of ducks made themselves at home on the small pond on the back acre.

Teaching reading and writing to local black people on Saturday afternoons fills my heart and gives me a reprieve from the house and the babies. Your idea was brilliant, and the Farnell's have convinced several local farmers to send their workers. The employers pay twenty-five cents per student per class on alternating weeks, and I have fourteen regular students. The barn loft is a good space for teaching.

I know I am doing something good for the community with my teaching. You were correct, as always, Wynston. Living for others is right living. We are richly blessed and ever grateful to you. We miss our evening talks with you already.

Sincerely,

Mitilde

Lena lowered the head of her bed and rested her eyes. Shivering with chills, she called the nurse, who checker her temperature, which was 100.4 degrees. The nurse brought Lena some ibuprofen and apple juice.

Lena's mind spun as she sipped the apple juice. If her great-grandmother Willi really was Wynston Jamison Panton's biological daughter, then she and Gwyn were related – if only distantly and by marriage – to Ria. This would be difficult to explain to Ria, not to mention David and Ben. Before allowing herself to rest, Lena sent a text to Gwyn.

> Just finished reading the letters. Struggling to process all of this. How could I possibly explain this to Ria? Fever back up. Am tired and overwhelmed – nap time.

> You don't need to worry about explaining things to Ria. I told her and Ben everything we have learned. We are going to ride snowmobiles to the hospital since the roads are bad – bringing dinner later. Everything is fine. Sweet dreams.

Growing increasingly heavy, Lena's eyelids became more difficult to open. She pulled the blankets over her head and closed her eyes. Feverish, overwhelmed, and too tired to worry about how Ria, David, and Ben would react, Lena slept soundly for several hours.

The rhythmic squeaking of Gwyn's wet rubber snow boots on the floor of her hospital room awakened Lena. Gwyn was dressed in a hooded full-body snowmobile suit and had ski goggles on her forehead. As she fumbled with the remote and raised the head of her hospital bed, Lena informed her sister that she looked like one of the cartoon power rangers.

"Hey, sis," Gwyn said breathlessly as she removed her backpack. "Brrr! It is *really* nasty out there! We already have two feet of snow, and it is dumping." Gwyn shook the snow from her hood in Lena's direction.

"Hey yourself," Lena replied as she reached for her purple Colorado Rockies baseball cap. She pulled her long brown hair through the opening in the back of the cap. "Would you mind bringing me a cool wet washcloth? I must look awful. Are Ria and Ben coming?"

"Ben and Ria are downstairs so we can have a couple of minutes alone – they will be up in a few minutes." Gwyn went to the bathroom and moistened a washcloth, which she placed on Lena's forehead. Frowning, she said "You still have a fever, Lena. I brought you a bacon, lettuce, tomato, and avocado pita. Do you feel like you can eat right now?"

Lena shook her head. "I am tired of being still and feeling awful, Gwyn. I am also worried. How is Ria? How did your conversation go?"

"With everything you are dealing with I did not want disclosure to be a stressor for you, Lena, so I just handled it honestly. I hope you don't mind." Gwyn eyed her sister with concern.

"Now who is the big sister?" Lena asked with a slight grin.

"I learned from the very best. Anyhow, here is the scoop. Ria is very intrigued by it all – more surprised and curious than anything. Ben was quiet for most of the time. He seemed a little suspicious, frankly, but after a while he started talking about spirit guides and destiny. I think he is okay – sort of a 21st century hippy, isn't he?"

Smiling, Lena squeezed her sister's hand. "Yes, he is. I am grateful you told them the truth. Thank you."

"Anyway," Gwyn continued, "I had a dream about Mitilde. She told me to look inside her Bible, so Ria and I went back to the garret this afternoon. The Bible was still there in the bottom drawer of the dresser." Gwyn pulled an old Bible from the backpack and handed it to Lena. "Open it."

Lena opened the Bible gently. The blank first page contained an inscription in intricate, feminine cursive. Lena read it aloud.

12 August 1885

This Bible presented to Mitilde S. Freeman

on the occasion of your Baptism

and

in celebration of the completion of your

literacy and nursing education.

Gen. & Mrs. W. J. Panton

An old, folded piece of paper lay inside the front cover. Opening the folded paper carefully, Lena was surprised to see a fragile lock of black hair tied with a faded ribbon. Lena read the letter aloud.

Dear Mitilde:

It is with great sadness that I write to inform you of your mother's passing. The tuberculosis took her this morning, the 6th of May 1888. I am sending you this lock of your mother's hair in hopes it will bring you some comfort. She was proud to know you were earning an education and looked forward to your letters. I would read them to her when they arrived each week. We will provide a proper burial for Awah at Sharp Street Cemetery.

My Deepest Condolences,

Gertrude Panton

"Oh my… it is true!" Lena stared at the letter in disbelief. "If Mitilde's mother's name was Awah, then it must be true. Uncle Billy's letter said that our great-great grandmother Mitilde's mother was named Awah. This is all just too much."

"Lena, I am thinking that with that lock of hair, we might be able to get a DNA test to see if we really are related to Mitilde's mother, Awah" Gwyn said.

"Did someone say DNA test?" Will Winslow smiled as he strode confidently into the room. "We have a DNA lab here at the hospital, you know. Most results come back in 24 to 72 hours."

While Gwyn was explaining to Will some of the most significant occurrences and discoveries since their arrival at Glen Eyrie Castle, Ria and Ben entered the room. Will suggested that since Lena was having blood drawn twice daily, it might be possible to run a DNA test against the lock of hair because there appeared to be several strands of hair in the lock that had intact roots. Lena remembered that the old hot comb in the maid's quarters had several intact hairs in its bristles that might also be helpful. Will asked Lena if she wanted him to order the test, but he received no response.

Lena's expression was blank, and she was staring at the far corner of the room. Gwyn, Ben, and Ria were all perfectly still, staring at the same spot. Will followed their gazes to the dark corner where five women spirits stood side by side. Three of the spirits appeared to be Black, and each appeared to be from a different period. Seemingly frozen, Will could only stare with the others in disbelief until the women slowly faded.

"OK… we, um… we all just saw a group of ghosts over there in the corner, right?" Ben asked in a hushed whisper. Everyone nodded. "Wonder who they were?"

"I *know* who they were," Gwyn said, wiping a tear from her cheek. "My mother, my Granny M., her mother Wilhelmina Thomas, Wilhelmina's mother Mitilde Thomas, and her mother Awah Freeman."

Will looked at Lena, who met his gaze. Her eyes brimming with tears, Lena nodded as she wiped feverish perspiration from her brow. Ria sat down on the bed next to Lena and took her hand. "Lena, I encourage you to do the DNA test – I will gladly go get the hot comb from the maid's room and bring it here to the hospital. You deserve to know the truth. We all do. This set of circumstances is really strange, to say the least. But maybe if we can expose the truth then the spirits at Glen Eyrie and the spirits of your ancestors can rest."

Chapter Ten Recipes

BLTA Pitas

    3 c. lettuce, shredded or chopped

    1 Roma tomato, finely chopped

    8 slices bacon, fried and crumbled

    1 ripe avocado, finely chopped

    3 T mayonnaise

    2 T AJ's ® Walla Walla Sweet Onion Mustard

    ½ t. ground pepper

Directions:

1. Fry bacon, drain, and crumble.

2. In a bowl combine all ingredients and mix well.

3. Spoon mixture into pita pocket halves.

— CHAPTER 11 —

A Busy Knight

Feeling clear-headed and refreshed, Lena knew when she awoke on Thursday morning that she was improving. Two nurses helped her into a wheelchair, removed the bandages from her feet, and took her to a wheel-in shower stall where she could wash herself. Marveling at the simple luxury of a private bathing experience, Lena was especially grateful for the Crabtree & Evelyn body wash, shampoo, and lotion that Gwyn had bought for her from the hospital gift shop.

Lena was grateful to see Gwyn waiting for her when she returned to her room. Once she was settled back in the bed, Lena applied some lip gloss and mascara using a small handheld mirror. Gwyn combed some shine drops and a light styling gel through Lena's long chestnut brown hair. Then she blew it dry and used a flat iron to create loose beachy waves.

"Thanks, Gwyn. I feel *sooo* much better and am sure I look better, too." Lena said quietly. She sipped the last of the breakfast smoothie Gwyn had brought for her and rested her head against the pillow. "I cannot believe that taking a shower and sitting up while you did my hair took so much energy. My body is going to require me to sleep again for a little while."

Gwyn lowered the head of Lena's bed and pulled the sheet and blankets over her. "In case I don't tell you enough, I love you, Lena. You scared me this week. You and Uncle Billy and Aunt Becky are the only family I have left. You know, I would be terribly lost without you." Gwyn's voice cracked, and she blinked away the tears that clouded her eyes.

"I love you, too, sis" Lena said drowsily as her sister squeezed her hand. By the time Gwyn drew the curtains and turned out the lights, Lena was asleep. Gwyn put the hair styling tools and products into Lena's overnight bag in the small closet in the corner of the room. Then, deciding to catch a quick nap herself, she settled into the reclining chair next to Lena's bed and covered herself with her winter coat.

Lena was awakened by someone gently rubbing her forearm. It was Ben, who had stopped by with his sons to say goodbye before heading back to Elk Mountain Ranch. Gwyn stood up, stretched, and decided to take the young boys to the cafeteria for lunch so Ben and Lena could have some time alone. Ben pulled a rolling stool up next to Lena's bed and smiled. "You look better," he said.

"The miracle of makeup," Lena said as she raised the head of her bed. "I do feel better today. Ben, you didn't have to leave the tour because of me, you know."

"Oh, please! Ria and David both insisted," he said. "Ria was beside herself when Calvin told her you had passed out and were in intensive care. Truth is, we don't see much of David when he is on tour, anyway." Ben smiled at her affectionately. "I told you the castle was haunted Lena. But honestly – I would never have encouraged you to have anything to do with the place if I had known the spirits would hurt you. I feel so responsible for what has happened to you. I am terribly sorry."

"What happened was no one's fault." Lena squeezed Ben's hand and looked at him seriously. "Now listen. It is important to me that you understand something. I want you to know that I had no idea about any of these possible connections to Ria's family until the past 24 hours, Ben. More than likely the DNA test will prove there is no relation between us, and we will be laughing about this crazy set of coincidences for years. I hope this situation will not negatively impact our friendship. You and your family are dear to me. Your friendship is a gift."

"I believe you, and I treasure your friendship. So does Ben. But Lena, you are kidding yourself if you do not believe that General Panton is your however-many-greats grandfather. I mean, think about it - all of the clues, the information from your uncle, the letter in Mitilde's Bible – it just adds up. Then last night everyone who was in this room – including *a doctor* - saw five generations of your female ancestors standing right there" he said, pointing at the corner. "Lena, open your eyes!"

"I'm sorry, Ben. I still do not feel well, and all the medications they have me on make processing this information incredibly difficult. The truth is that I am really struggling right now physically and intellectually." Lena sighed deeply. "Honestly, I would give anything for you to say something unrelated to my accident or this whole situation - something that will make me laugh."

Determined to do exactly that, Ben changed the subject and told Lena about David's tour and the boys' latest pranks. "Last week they unwrapped a candy bar and put it in the shallow end of the swimming pool at the hotel. We had no idea until some lady screamed that there was a turd in the pool. There we were at the Ritz- Carlton in Los Angeles, waiting for someone to clean the pool, when Luke yells '*Ha-ha fooled you!*' It was impossible not to laugh because we *knew* it was a prank, but no one else at the pool thought it was funny at all. Then somehow a couple of nights ago they slipped grapes in David's underwear while he was sleeping, and he woke up in a sticky mess!"

Laughing, Lena said, "Goodness, I'm starting to regret that I never had brothers. They sound like a handful of fun! Thank you for making me smile, Ben. I really needed a good laugh." Ben gave Lena an affectionate hug and made her promise to follow the doctors' instructions. He assured her that the roads were passable and promised to send her a text once he and the boys arrived safely at Elk Mountain Ranch.

Will arrived with another doctor, so Ben left to find Gwyn and the boys in the cafeteria. Will approached the side of the bed and met her eyes. "You look great, Lena. Your temperature is normal, and your white count looks good, so I've arranged for you to be transferred to the inpatient rehabilitation unit this afternoon."

Will introduced the other doctor as his dear friend and colleague, Dr. Monte Jarret. Dr Jarrett would be taking over Lena's care. "A pleasure to meet you, Ms. Thomas" Dr. Jarrett said. "May I call you Lena?" Lena nodded. "If all goes well your stitches will come out early next week. After that, physical therapy will work with you on a plan to get you back on your feet. With any luck, you'll be discharged as early as next Wednesday or Thursday."

Dr. Jarret left, and Gwyn returned as Will set his clipboard on the counter and sat on the side of Lena's bed. He looked at Gwyn, then at Lena and sighed. "I am a doctor. I work in a hospital. I have seen a lot of crazy things. Not many people know this, but hospitals are hotbeds for paranormal activity. I have seen spirits in the past, but I have never seen five generations of spirits at one time, and I have never heard of spirits physically harming human beings before. To be honest, Lena, I am concerned for your safety."

Lena assured Will that while the ghosts were unnerving, even frightening, she felt confident that most of the spirits were protective in nature. Gwyn suggested that the sleepwalking incident, based on some Internet research she had done that morning, might have been caused by a heightened sensitivity to spirit energy.

Laughing at Gwyn's comment, Lena said, "A week ago I would have told you that I didn't believe in this sort of nonsense! Now, though, I don't suppose I have much choice."

Will's shift did not start until 10:00 the following morning, so he asked if Lena would have coffee with him. Lena agreed, and he promised to bring her a nonfat vanilla latte from his favorite local coffee shop. They exchanged cell phone numbers, and Lena promised to call him if she needed anything. Before Will left he handed her a small, squarish plastic bottle. "Holy water," he said. "Compliments of the hospital chaplain. Even if you are not Catholic, I think you should keep this with you."

Ding. The text notification on Lena's phone sounded. Will squeezed her hand, gazed into Lena's eyes briefly, then smiled as he stood up and left the room. Lena looked at her phone and saw that the text message was from Jasmyn.

Lena, no one at work will tell me anything. It isn't my business, but I really care about you. Are you doing any better?
Jasmyn

Yesterday was hard, but I am doing much better today. Being transferred to the inpatient rehab unit this afternoon.

I am so relieved! Can I come to see you this weekend? BTW this morning I finally got time to watch the video footage of the knight in the foyer from last Friday. Two crazy things happened! The files are large, so I emailed them to you. Watch them right away!

Intrigued to see what might have been captured by the camera, Gwyn handed Lena her laptop and sat on the side of the bed. Lena opened the e-mail from Jasmyn and clicked on the first link. The clip started at 12:54 a.m. and was 17 seconds long; the camera's night vision technology enabled them to see the foyer and the knight clearly. At six seconds the knight's face shield slowly opened, causing the same metal-on-metal sound the women had heard on their first evening at Glen Eyrie. At 13 seconds the large iron knight shifted slightly to the right, in the direction of the main reception hall. The sisters watched the clip twice and agreed there was nothing visible in the clip that would have caused either movement.

The second link in Jasmyn's e-mail was a longer clip nearly two and a half minutes long. It started at 3:03 a.m. Twelve seconds into the video clip the pocket doors leading to the General's smoking room to the left of the knight opened fully. At 18 seconds a white mist emerged from the smoking room and disappeared into the back of the iron knight. Thirty-one seconds into the clip the knight's right arm raised and the sisters watched in shock as the red flower in its hand floated into the air and slowly disappeared through the upper right corner of the screen.

One minute and 12 seconds into the clip, the knight's right hand lowered to its original position. Three seconds later the knight's face shield closed. Fifteen seconds after the face shield closed, the knight's position shifted abruptly to the left, returning to the position it had been in the beginning of the first clip. At one minute and 44 seconds, a white mist emerged from the front of the knight and slowly disappeared into the General's smoking room. At two minutes and 21 seconds, the pocket doors closed.

Lena played the clip again, pausing it at one minute and 47 seconds. She zoomed in on the white mist and sucked in her breath. "Gwyn, do you see what I see?"

Gwyn picked up the laptop and inspected the frozen image closely. "It is faint, but I can see a short butler's coat, which could mean that Charles' spirit is causing the knight to move! Maybe he is still trying to protect the castle or the General."

Nodding, Lena replied, "Or maybe he knew who we were and was trying to get our attention."

While Gwyn packed Lena's bags in anticipation of her relocation to the inpatient rehabilitation unit, Lena texted Jasmyn.

WOW! I can't believe it. Freeze the image in the second clip at 1:47. What do you see?

Looks like a short jacket – I did not see that before! Since the door to the butler's quarters is in the smoking room, I bet you a latte the butler is protecting the place. Like he is still serving the general in some way!

That is our theory, too. I would love to see you, but please don't make the trip down unless you're also coming to see that handsome security guard. Dilbert seems nice.

DILLON, not Dilbert! OMG. And yes, that is the plan. He is an amazing kisser.

That is not the sort of information a person normally shares with their boss – TMI and gross!

☺ Sorry not sorry. See you tomorrow or Saturday!

That afternoon Lena settled into her new room in the inpatient rehabilitation unit. The room was surprisingly comfortable and offered a comfortable brown leather recliner for guests, where Gwyn spent much of the afternoon. Lena especially appreciated the soft glow provided by two wall sconces and a floor lamp because she had grown to despise the overhead fluorescent lighting in her hospital room. After physical therapy, hydrotherapy and fresh bandages, Lena was tired and hungry. The rehabilitation unit was much quieter than the hospital room, and the comfortable décor of the room helped Lena to relax. She responded to several work e-mails, and then allowed herself to go to sleep early.

At the carriage house that evening Gwyn found herself alone with Ria for the first time. Though she maintained a calm and gracious exterior, she could not help but feel somewhat defensive during the awkward string of direct questions Ria directed at her. Gwyn decided she really could not blame the woman for being suspicious, so she answered each of Ria's questions honestly, patiently, and thoroughly.

Over a dinner of homemade bacon macaroni and cheese, the women compared their strange experiences at the castle. Gwyn shared every detail of the last week with Ria, who seemed to appreciate being fully informed. Ria apologized for being harsh, and Gwyn assured Ria that she understood. Ria recalled several old family photo albums she had once seen in a cabinet in the castle library. The two women walked to the castle to retrieve the photo albums and a bottle of wine to pair with the orange ginger pound cake Gwyn had made for dessert.

"Spirits, we think we know the truth about Mitilde's babies." Ria shouted as they entered the castle foyer. "This is my friend Gwyn. We believe she may be a descendant of Wynston and Mitilde. We are here to retrieve some old family picture albums that might help us uncover the truth. Please, please do not scare us while we are here."

The castle was quiet, almost too quiet as far as Gwyn was concerned. Ria and Gwyn quickly ascended the main staircase and made their way to the second-floor library. Gwyn carried a hurricane lamp in her left hand in case the lights went out again, and Ria turned on lights as they made their way.

When the lights turned on in the library, the women noticed an ornate painted cabinet along the right wall with its doors ajar. Ria thanked the spirits for opening the cabinet and pulled out three large, leather-bound albums. Then she loudly informed the spirits they were going to get a bottle of wine from the cellar.

Gwyn had not been to the cellar before. She marveled at the stone walls, giant wood support beams, and countless bottles of wine. Ria told Gwyn that the Panton family had been fond of wine for several generations and shared that James had been an international wine distributor. As Ria reached for the light switch to the wine room, a slight cool breeze swirled around the women. A male voice whispered, *I love you, Ria. Do not fear the truth.*

"James? My darling is that you?" Ria fought back tears. *Yes, my love. I am with you always. Find your happiness again.* Ria collapsed to her knees and the cold air encircled her, as if in an embrace. She buried her face in her hands and cried. Gwyn set the hurricane lamp on the floor and knelt beside Ria. When Ria was ready, Gwyn helped her to her feet. The woman was trembling too hard to navigate the stairs, so they sat together in silence on the cellar stairs for several minutes.

"Please tell me you heard him, Gwyn" Ria pleaded. Gwyn nodded her head affirmatively.

"He is right, you know." Ria finally said. "Memories of being James' wife, raising Melissa, and my job with David are all that keep me here in Colorado. Melissa has been asking me to come live with her family in Japan. I would love to be with my daughter and twin grandsons. Maybe it would help me heal." Gwyn rubbed Ria's back gently.

"I can't imagine your grief" Gwyn said softly. "I lost my fiancé to a motorcycle accident several years ago, but I am sure that losing your spouse after so many years together is devastating. For what it is worth, I think you should do what is right for you, Ria. The rest will work itself out."

Ria gave Gwyn a grateful hug and suggested they grab a second bottle of wine before heading back to the carriage house. They chose a 1966 Suduiraut and a 1990 old tawny dessert wine to pair with the ginger orange pound cake. As they ascended the cellar stairs, Gwyn asked Ria if she thought twins might be a Panton family trait. Ria agreed it was a possibility.

As the two women walked back to the carriage house, Gwyn heard neighing and the sound of quickly approaching galloping horses. She shined her flashlight in the direction of the approaching horses, but as she did so the sound vanished, and she could not see any movement.

"You won't see them… at least I never have." Ria said. "There haven't been horses on the property since Melissa was a child, but I do hear them like this from time to time."

"Ghost horses?" Gwyn asked as her heart raced. Ria nodded and nudged Gwyn in the direction of the carriage house.

Pairing the Suduirau wine with her pound cake was as close to perfect as a chef could hope for in Gwyn's opinion. Ria, who fancied herself a 'certifiable foodie,' agreed. While savoring their dessert, Gwyn and Ria leafed through pages of aged photographs.

Numerous labelled old photos in the albums confirmed that the male ghost seen over the past week was indeed General Panton, the woman in the blue dress was Queenie, and the brunette spirit in the white dress Gwyn had seen was their eldest daughter, Evalynn. There were no pictures of the maid or the butler in any of the albums.

While she struggled to uncork the bottle of dessert wine, Gwyn told Ria about the video clips Jasmyn had sent and asked if she would like to watch them. Ria nodded, so Gwyn set up her laptop and opened the e-mail Lena had forwarded. While Ria watched the clips, Gwyn won her battle with the stubborn cork and filled two glasses with the old tawny wine.

"Stop it at one minute, 47 seconds and zoom in on the misty thing" Gwyn said as Ria clicked on the link to the second video. Ria watched the video all the way through, then watched it again, pausing as Gwyn had directed. Stunned, Ria said she could barely make out a man's short-waisted jacket. Gwyn confirmed that is what she and Lena thought, and was the reason they she believed the mist to be the spirit of the butler, Charles Thomas.

Ria confessed that the idea of the butler being responsible for the knight's occasional movement had never occurred to her; she had always assumed it was an ancient warrior who was still attached to his battle gear. Enjoying a buzz from the wine, the two women talked for hours about the spirits, grief, and the events of the week. Shortly after 10:30 p.m. Gwyn's phone rang.

"Hi Aunt Becky. It is awfully late there – is everything OK?" Ria knew something was wrong as she listened to Gwyn's side of the conversation. When Gwyn hung up the phone and she sank onto the antique camelback settee in Ria's living room in stunned silence. Ria handed her a tissue and put her arm around Gwyn's shoulders as tears slowly fell down Gwyn's face.

"My Uncle Billy had a massive stroke and died tonight. He and my aunt Becky are the only close family Lena and I have left. Oh, God, Ria. How am I going to tell Lena? I don't think she can take much more, I really don't!" Gwyn dabbed at her eyes with a tissue, overcome with shock and grief.

A movement in her peripheral vision caught Gwyn's attention. She turned to her left and looked behind the sofa. There stood the full-body apparition of her beloved Uncle Billy. He was smiling at her, somehow slightly transparent and luminescent at the same time. Noting Gwyn's shocked expression, Ria followed Gwyn's gaze.

"Is… is that your uncle?" Ria whispered, grasping Gwyn's hand tightly. Gwyn nodded slightly.

Do not worry, Gwyn, I am just fine. Look in the family file on my computer. Wynston and Mitilde want their secret to be revealed. The apparition vanished in the blink of an eye, though the distinct smell of Uncle Billy's Sutliff pipe tobacco lingered in the air for several minutes.

Chapter Eleven Recipes

Bacon Mac 'n Cheese

    16 oz elbow macaroni

    8 slices applewood bacon

    ¼ c. butter or margarine

    4 T flour

    3 ½ c. milk

    1 t. salt

    1 t. pepper

    1 ½ t. Penzey's ® Tuscan Sunset Italian Seasoning

    ¼ t. cayenne

    4 T. Dijon mustard

    2 ¼ c. sharp cheddar cheese, shredded

    ½ c. parmesan cheese, shredded

    ¼ c. Velveeta, diced

    〜

    1/2 c butter

    1 c Panko Japanese style breadcrumbs

    ½ t garlic salt

    Paprika

Directions:

1. Cook macaroni to al dente according to instructions on the package.

2. While macaroni is cooking, fry the bacon, then set on paper towels to absorb grease. When cool, chop or crumble into bits.

3. In a saucepan over medium heat, melt ¼ cup butter. When butter is melted, add flour, and whisk to make a roux.

4. When roux is thick, add milk slowly while whisking.

5. Add mustard and seasonings to mixture, whisk well.

6. Add cheese. Stir occasionally over medium heat until the cheese is completely melted, and the mixture begins to thicken.

7. Drain macaroni and put in a large casserole dish.

8. Pour cheese mixture over macaroni and stir well.

9. Preheat oven to 350 degrees.

10. Melt ½ c butter in frying pan over medium-high heat. When melted, add garlic salt and breadcrumbs. Brown, then sprinkle evenly over the top of the macaroni.

11. Sprinkle paprika over dish.

12. Bake for 35 minutes.

— CHAPTER 12 —

As It Should Be

Will arrived Friday morning with coffee and a small bouquet of yellow roses and white daisies tucked into a yellow happy face mug. He was pleased to see Lena sitting upright in a wheelchair reading the issue of *Colorado Homes & Lifestyles* magazine he had bought for her.

"Good morning, lovely lady" he said, flashing her a crooked smile.

"You're looking lovely yourself!" Lena said, accepting the flowers. "These are so cheerful – thank you! I have to admit, I woke up grumpy today."

Will handed her a coffee and made himself comfortable in the chair. "Well, that's a sign you're getting better. How are the feet?" He pulled her wheelchair toward him until their knees touched, then reached up and brushed a stray curl from Lena's forehead.

Savoring a sip of her latte, Lena pondered her response. "They are itchy. They would like to stand up, and maybe even walk." Will distracted her by recommending local places he would take her for a date if she could walk. Lena decided that the Winery at Holy Cross Abbey and the Royal Gorge bridge sounded like the places she would most like to see, and they agreed that their first date would be a visit to the winery once Lena was back on her feet.

Will's eyes met hers, and the two studied each other for a moment. "Dr. Winslow, may I ask what you are thinking about?" Lena asked curiously.

"To be completely honest I am thinking about how strange it is that we haven't even been on a date yet, but I would still really like to kiss you" he replied, somewhat sheepishly.

Lena smiled and shifted her eyes downward. "Funny" she said, "I was just thinking about how much I wish you would kiss me." Will stood up from the chair and bent over the wheelchair. He took Lena's face in his hands, and pressed his lips gently to hers, allowing them to linger.

"Ahem!" The sound of Gwyn clearing her throat from the door to Lena's room provided an unwelcome interruption to an otherwise lovely moment.

Gwyn's swollen eyes and somewhat disheveled appearance took Lena by surprise. "What's wrong?" Lena asked with concern.

Gwyn stood motionless in the doorway. "It's Uncle Billy" Gwyn said. "He had a stroke last night."

Lena's heart fell. "Oh, no. Gwyn, please tell me he is alright." She waited for Gwyn to respond, though in her heart she already knew the truth.

Gwyn closed her eyes and shook her head. "I can't, Lena. I'm sorry. Uncle Billy is gone." Certain that her heart might break, Lena bowed her head, covered her mouth with her right hand, and closed her eyes as Will placed a firm, comforting hand on her shoulder.

Will stayed with Gwyn and Lena for the next hour, listening to the sisters share favorite memories of their uncle. At 10:15 he stood up and gathered his things. "Your uncle sounds like a fine man. I apologize, but my shift starts in 15 minutes. How about I make sure that any therapy appointments scheduled for this morning are rescheduled for the afternoon?"

Lena nodded and squeezed his hand. "I know this isn't what you probably had in mind for our coffee date this morning, Will. But I am glad you were here, and I'm really thankful that you stayed with us for a while."

Putting his white coat on as he walked to the door, Will smiled and said, "It wasn't so bad. I got to kiss the best-looking woman for miles around. The pleasure was mine, even though we got caught by your kid sister!" With a wink and a mischievous smile, he left the room and closed the door.

Following a call to their Aunt Becky, Lena insisted that Gwyn fly to Georgia to support their aunt and help with Uncle Billy's final arrangements. She logged into her Freedom Airlines frequent flyer account and used accumulated travel points to purchase her sister a flight departing Denver International Airport the following day. Encouraged by her sister's condition and confident she was receiving excellent care, Gwyn reluctantly left to head back to Denver so she could pack for the trip.

The afternoon brought a little freedom for Lena. She was delighted to finally be free from both oxygen and the IV, but desperately wished she could walk. She was determined during her physical therapy appointment and thankful for the soothing warmth of a hydrotherapy session for her feet. A late afternoon visit from Jasmyn lifted Lena's spirits. Jasmyn brought two of her mother's homemade tamales for Lena, as well as some paperwork from Chamberlain International Realty. The young intern was excited for her evening plans – she was having dinner and going to an escape room with Dillon.

Jasmyn also brought Lena a gift from her parents, a Saint Michael medal. "We are Catholic," Jasmyn explained. "In our faith tradition Saint Michael represents the battle between good and evil. In the book of Revelations, St. Michael fights and defeats Satan. So, when we fear evil, we pray to Saint Michael to protect us. My parents had this medal blessed by our parish priest specifically for you. Please keep it with you for protection, Lena. There is a copy of the Saint Michael Prayer in the box underneath the prayer."

Lena smiled fondly at Jasmyn. "Honestly, Jasmyn, I think this is the most thoughtful gift I have ever received, and it means the world to me. Please thank your family for me. I will keep this with me and treasure it always." Jasmyn shared her excitement about getting to know Dillon, and Lena made the intern promise that if the roads were too icy or if she had too much to drink, she would come stay the night in the recliner in Lena's room.

"I promise, Lena." Jasmyn turned to leave, but then stopped in the doorway. She turned around and faced Lena. "I hope this doesn't sound unprofessional, Lena, but I want you to know that I care a lot about you. I look up to you, and I am just so thankful you are feeling better. I have been praying for you every day."

"Thank you, Jasmyn. I care about you, too, and I am grateful for your prayers. You know, you remind me a lot of myself when I was younger. I'm really proud of who you are, and I can only imagine how proud your parents must be." Lena winked at the young woman. "Now go have some fun with that cute blond Dilbert guy!"

"Oh, geez!" Jasmyn rolled her eyes. "Dillon! His name is Dillon, not Dilbert, you big weirdo!" Jasmyn blew a kiss in Lena's direction and pulled on her gloves before leaving and closing the door softly behind her.

Grateful for a relatively quiet weekend, Lena accomplished some work-related tasks. She received regular updates from Gwyn and enjoyed daily visits with Will, whose presence was comfortable and calming for Lena. Their long talks revealed the two shared interests in skiing, wine, good food, and history. Lena shared everything about the events of the past week with Will, who said his father concurred with Lena that the spirits at Glen Eyrie Castle were restless, but more than likely harmless.

Dr. Jarrett stopped by late Sunday afternoon with results of the DNA test. The comparison of the lock of hair from Mitilde's Bible and the hairs from Mitilde's hot comb with Lena's blood confirmed that Lena was a blood relative to both the person to whom the lock of hair belonged and the person to whom the hair in the hot comb belonged.

Lena called Gwyn to share the information. Gwyn said she suspected their uncle would have figured everything out before long because the information she found in the *Family* folder from Uncle Billy's desktop traced back to Mitilde. Uncle Billy had identified Charles Thomas as Mitilde's husband and father of Marie and Wilhelmina and had also confirmed that Mitilde had worked in Colorado for General Panton.

Gwyn said that Uncle Billy's remains were to be cremated, but that their Aunt Becky was not willing to discuss a funeral yet. Becky insisted on speaking to Lena on the phone and seemed reassured that Lena was doing better. Before hanging up, Gwyn reminded Lena to rest her mind and her body.

Recognizing the wisdom in Gwyn's advice, Lena closed her laptop and set it on the nightstand table. She turned off the lights and was about to silence her cell phone for the night when a text message from Ria came in.

> Sorry I did not come visit this weekend. I will explain tomorrow. Gwyn told me about the test results – I can call you "cousin" now! 😊 What is a good time to come by tomorrow?

> Ria, I had thought I would share that information with you personally – I'm sorry. And yes, I suppose we are distant cousins! The physical therapist will be done torturing me at 11:00. Sometime mid-afternoon?

> Perfect. I am bringing my attorney with me. You, your sister, and your aunt are entitled to a portion of the estate. We have spent the past two days figuring out a plan that we would like to share with you.

> Ria, that is NOT necessary. The estate is yours and yours alone.

> James visited me, and I have clarity now. It is only right, Lena. Please don't think about it for another minute until I get there tomorrow. Get some rest!

Monday morning Dr. Jarret told Lena she would be getting her stitches out on Tuesday, and that she would begin some light weight-bearing exercises with physical therapy. If she progressed well, Lena would be released Tuesday afternoon or Wednesday morning. She would need a walker for a couple of days and could then progress to using crutches until her feet were sufficiently healed to bear her full weight.

Although Lena was ecstatic about being released and regaining some independence, she knew she would not be able to live independently for at least a couple of weeks. Lena called Gwyn, who suggested she research home nursing care, at least until Gwyn returned Friday evening. Lena was researching home nursing care when Will arrived with coffee.

Lena brought Will up to speed regarding the DNA test results, the texts from Ria, and Lena's potential release from the inpatient rehabilitation unit. Will said home nursing care was not a bad idea, but suggested that she stay with him, at least until Gwyn could return to Colorado Springs on Saturday. "I am off on Wednesday and can get my shifts covered through Saturday, though it is possible I could be called in on an emergency. I don't cook as well as your sister, but I promise I would take good care of you."

Surprised by Will's suggestion Lena considered the possibility while she studied Will's face. She had known him only eight days, but she was so comfortable with Will that at moments he seemed a natural extension of herself. "Will, we've only just met and I'm practically an invalid. That's far too much to ask but thank you."

"Please think about it, Lena" he said. He lifted her chin and placed a gentle kiss on her lips. "It is a selfish request. The truth is I would love to spend some time with you, so I do not want you to go back to Denver. Besides, you would have a doctor with you 24/7 until Gwyn gets here. It will buy you time to figure things out. Just promise me you will think about it, ok? Let me know by 3:00 so I can arrange to have my shifts covered if I need to." Lena agreed.

The physical therapy room was full of strange equipment, but despite her initial intimidation she approached the appointment with determination. Lena learned to lift herself from the wheelchair onto a toilet seat using arm strength, a reclaimed sense of independence she had not anticipated but welcomed gratefully. Then she was strapped into a halter that supported most of her weight and placed just above the ground. There Lena practiced walking with the careful guidance of an occupational therapist and physical support from a physical therapist. She supported herself with her arms using two waist-high parallel bars, and the therapist supported her from behind.

Though walking even with so little weight cause her feet to tingle fiercely, Lena let out a loud *woohoo* as she reached the end of the rails, then she settled back fully into the harness seat and threw both arms straight into the air as if to signal a touchdown. The occupational therapist laughed and applauded, and a second set of applauding hands also celebrated Lena's effort. Lena turned to see Will leaning casually against the wall holding a Victoria's Secret shopping bag, grinning widely.

"Hello, Dr. Winslow" the physical therapist said. Will came up behind Lena, wrapped his arms around her waist in the harness and planted a kiss on her ear.

"Atta girl, beautiful" he whispered into Lena's ear. "You two taking good care of my lady? Don't go cutting her any slack, you hear?"

"Oh, you're a couple!" exclaimed the physical therapist. "Yes, Will, we are being sufficiently rigorous, but if you like we can make her do it all again. And, if I may say so, the two of you make a lovely pair."

"Thank you, and you may say that anytime you like!" Will exclaimed. "Lena, I heard they'll be letting you wear something other than a hospital gown starting today, so I brought you something comfy to wear." He handed the shopping bag to her. "You up for some Chinese food? If so, I can order it delivered at 12:30 so you have time to get dressed."

Lena shot him a coy look. "You mean you want me to miss out on the *wonderful* hospital lunch I was *sooo* looking forward to? Yes! Moo shu chicken if they have it, please! Thank you, Will."

With a nod of his head Will departed. Following a warm shower, Lena put on the smooth pink silk pajama set that Will had purchased for her. It seemed an oddly intimate gift given the newness of their relationship, yet Lena relished the soft fabric against her skin. She was seated comfortably in the brown leather reclining chair while a nurse slathered a smooth substance on the soles of her feet when Will arrived for lunch.

He inspected her feet before the nurse wrapped them with gauze. "They look great, Lena. You really got lucky."

Over lunch Lena chattered excitedly about being able to wear clothes and her eagerness for some mobility. Will asked whether she had considered his offer to come stay at his place for a few days. "I really just want you to be careful, and it isn't advisable for you to be alone quite yet."

Lena tilted her head to one side and said, "We've known each other only a week, Will. Already you have bought me silk pajamas and invited me to stay at your place. I like you... a lot. I'd hate to mess things up by moving too fast."

"We can keep it strictly platonic, Lena" Will replied. He covered his pinky with his thumb and held the three middle fingers of his hand up and together. "Scout's honor – really!"

"Let's not make promises we might not keep, Scout" Lena replied with a chuckle. "Can I let you know after I speak with Ria this afternoon?"

Will feigned an offended expression. "Lena Thomas, what sort of boy do you think I am?" Lena smirked, embarrassed that she had spoken her mind. "Tell you what, Lena. We are adults. Let's not worry about tradition or anything other than what feels right for us. I promise not to pressure you in any way - you have plenty to deal with right now." He covered her with the faux fur blanket before returning to work, and Lena decided to take a nap.

Again, Lena dreamt of walking through the aspen grove near Glen Eyrie Castle. The small shrubs were in full bloom, and the vibrant red Indian paintbrush flowers were plentiful. She was walking hand-in-hand with a man. Lena placed her hand on her stomach and looked down. She could see that she was wearing jeans and her favorite hiking boots. The man pulled her gently toward him. When she looked up, Lena realized she was looking into the eyes of Will Winslow.

"Wake up, cousin." Lena's dream was interrupted by Ria, who was gently rubbing her hand. Ria's attorney stood behind her. He was a chubby, balding man with unusually long sideburns. He was wearing high-water khaki pants, a yellow argyle sweater over a white collared shirt, and a brown bow tie.

To Lena, Ria looked radiant and noticeably younger than she had appeared recently. Ria explained that she had decided to move to Japan to be with her daughter, son-in-law, and twin grandsons. While she would miss David, Ben, and their boys, she felt that being with her remaining family would help her to heal.

"Lena, Glen Eyrie is paid for. I have realized that I do not want or need the property. The remaining assets of the estate, including cash and holdings, are valued at $264 million. I would like to propose that $14 million be set aside for my grandsons. The remaining $250 million I believe should be split equally five ways between Melissa, myself, you, Gwyn, and your aunt."

Lena blinked rapidly, trying to comprehend what Ria was saying. "Ria, they gave me some pain medication after physical therapy. I think I am having trouble understanding this. I never asked for any part of the Glen Eyrie estate…"

Ria squeezed Lena's hand. "Just hear me out. General Panton was an incredible philanthropist. He donated much of his fortune to good causes when he was alive and was deeply committed to social justice, most notably in terms of equity for people of color and people with disabilities. It seems to me that Mitilde was marginalized both because of the color of her skin and her gender. Regardless of whether her relationship with the General was mutual, the truth is that for generations Black women were sexually and physically abused by White men."

Lena nodded in agreement, and Ria continued. "If you and I can agree on a plan to use Glen Eyrie in a manner that will benefit society, specifically marginalized people, in a meaningful way, then I will sell it to you and Gwyn at a very reasonable price. You said the assessor valued it at just under $42 million. If we can agree to a plan, I will sell it to you for $30 million, half of which I will put into a trust to help pay property taxes and maintenance on the place. There are a few items from the castle that I would like to have and pass down to Melissa and the twins, but aside from those few items I will sell the entire estate - the property, the castle, and all of its contents to you."

Dumbfounded, Lena glanced from Ria to the attorney, who stepped forward and set his briefcase on the table next to the recliner. He opened his briefcase and removed three manilla folders, then closed the briefcase, walked around the bed, and handed the folders to Lena.

"Regardless of whether you purchase the castle, my client has already signed legal papers to transfer cash payments to you, your sister, and your aunt, of $50 million each. The money will be paid in two installments, 50%

upon signature of the agreements, and 50% ninety days afterward. This provides us time to liquidate assets and move holdings. Do you understand?"

"I... I think so" Lena replied, blinking rapidly.

The man continued. "The estate was last audited 14 months ago. Full audit details are in each folder. Each folder contains an agreement for transfer of funds, which my client has already signed. In addition, your folder and your sister's folder contain a draft agreement articulating my client's offer to sell the castle to you for $30 million, half of which is to be invested to support the annual costs of maintaining the property. My client will sign that document if the three of you come to an agreement regarding the future of the property."

The man looked at Lena with a serious expression. "Ms. Thomas, I strongly encourage you to have an attorney look over these documents before you sign anything, especially given your present condition. Please have your attorney reach out to me directly if there are questions." The attorney placed a plaid wool driving cap on his balding head, tipped it slightly, and left the room.

Dumbfounded, Lena stared at Ria, who squeezed Lena's hand reassuringly. "Ria, there is absolutely no reason for you to do this – why in the world would you want to do this? I'm sorry, but I just do not understand."

"James came to me last night. He told me to make reparations by splitting the estate fairly, and to move on. He begged me to find happiness." Ria smiled, and though there were tears in the woman's eyes Lena sensed they were tears of relief.

"Lena, the estate is worth more money than I could ever possibly spend, and the castle has always seemed overwhelming and, well, downright *scary* to me. I'd like to come visit from time to time, but the simple truth is that I don't need it or want it personally." Ria smiled and sighed. "I haven't let David and Ben know yet, but today I will give them my resignation. I want to move to Japan to be with Melissa and the boys as soon as possible. If you and I can work things out, I would like to be in Japan by the end of March. Lena, it would bring me so much peace to know that Glen Eyrie would remain in family hands and that it was being used to benefit society. I think Queenie and the General might find some peace in that, too."

Lena looked at the manilla folders in her hands, and then at Ria. The financial figures boggled Lena's mind. She shook her head and tried to speak, but she was unable to find the right words, so she lowered her eyes and stared at the manilla folders in her hands.

"Lena, look!" Ria exclaimed. Lena looked up and saw that Ria was pointing toward the window. In the darkened corner next to the window stood Mitilde, with General Panton standing to her left and a slender, balding White man with in a short-waisted butler's coat standing to her right. All three figures were completely solid and wore peaceful smiles. Mitilde and the butler had their arms around one another's waists.

As it should be. Mitilde's voice was clear and strong. The butler nodded as the pair slowly faded. General Panton's spirit remained, though not as solid as it had initially been. Queenie's voice filled the room. *Thank you, Alexandria. Come Wynston, my beloved, it is time to go.* General Panton nodded, then vanished.

"Who... who is Alexandria?" Lena wondered aloud after she managed to catch her breath.

"That's me" Ria replied softly. "Ria is my nickname."

Chapter Twelve Recipes

Mrs. Diaz' Tamales

Four 16 oz bags of El Guapo Hojas Para Amal
    (corn husks for tamales)

2 lbs. ground pork

3 links chorizo sausage

¼ c. Crisco shortening

2 t. pepper

2 t. salt

½ t. cayenne

3 t. minced garlic

2 c. chicken bone broth

〜

2 lbs. frozen yellow corn, thawed

2 lbs. frozen white corn, thawed

1 chipotle pepper in adobo, pureed

¼ c. sugar

〜

1 ¼ c. Crisco shortening

¼ c. 14 Hands ® Hot to Trot red wine

2 sweet onions, peeled and finely diced

½ red onion, peeled and finely diced

1 jalapeno pepper, seeded and finely diced

1 each red, yellow, and green bell peppers, seeded and finely diced

1 can original Rotel, drained and pureed

2 jars Ibsa ® Pimientos Asados (peeled roasted pimento peppers)

2 t. Penzeys ® Tuscan Sunset seasoning

2 t. ground cumin

3 t. minced garlic

3 packets sazon goya seasoning

2 T. cornstarch

2 8-oz cans Contadina tomato sauce

Directions:

1. Rinse the corn husk leaves, remove silk, and place in a pot of boiling water. Turn heat to low and allow husks to soak for 4 hours. Replenish hot water regularly as needed.

2. Place ¼ cup Crisco in a large skillet and brown ground pork with cayenne, salt, pepper, and 3 t. of the minced garlic.

3. When ground pork is browned, add bone broth and sriracha. Cover and simmer until over medium-low heat for 30 minutes. Set aside and allow to cool.

4. Run thawed corn through a food processor on pulse to produce a thick, chunky mush. Empty into a bowl and stir in the sugar.

5. In a large pot melt 1 ¼ c. Crisco ® shortening over medium-high heat. Add the 3 t. minced garlic, peppers, pimientos asados, and onions. Cook until onions become translucent.

6. Add wine and pureed Rotel. Stir well. Return to a simmer.

7. Add corn mixture and the pureed chipotle in adobo. Stir well. Return to a simmer.

8. Reduce heat to medium. Add meat, tomato sauce, and remaining ingredients. When the mixture begins to simmer, reduce to medium-low heat and simmer uncovered for one hour or until excess liquid has cooked away. Stir frequently.

9. Using one corn husk as a pocket, fill ¾ full with filling. Wrap with a second husk, opposing ends and seams. Wrap lengthwise and widthwise with kitchen twine, so that each "packet" is secure, but the filling has some room to expand.

10. Set steamer rack over 2" of boiling water and stack tamales on the rack, exposed seam down.

11. Cover and simmer 45 minutes, replenishing water, as necessary. Remove when filling is set and allow to cool.

12. Husks are not intended to be eaten. Unpeel and dispose of corn husks before eating.

13. Tamales may be served warm or at room temperature but should not be allowed to sit out for more than 3 hours before being refrigerated.

— CHAPTER 13 —

Horses and a House Key

At Ria's encouragement, Lena agreed to stay in the guest room at the carriage house once she was discharged from the inpatient rehabilitation unit Tuesday afternoon. The one-story carriage house was easily accessible, and Lena needed time with Ria to figure out a way forward with the Panton estate. Staying at Will's house felt like a premature and risky step for Lena.

Concerned about being too much of a burden on Ria, Lena asked Will if he would stay with her at the carriage house. Will arranged to take half days at the hospital for the rest of the week. He planned to spend mornings and nights with Lena at the carriage house until Gwyn's return to Colorado Springs on Saturday morning.

Jonathan Stevens was one of Lena's few close friends. He worked as legal counsel for Chamberlain Internationally Realty and several other high-profile businesses in Denver. Jonathan's expertise in property law would be helpful and Lena knew he could be trusted, so she decided to ask for his help. Thankful when Jonathan answered her call early Tuesday morning, Lena explained her situation. Jonathan agreed to meet her at the carriage house late Wednesday afternoon to review the legal documents Ria's attorney had provided.

Nervous about having her stitches taken out and simultaneously eager to reclaim some mobility and independence, Lena was dressed in leggings and her favorite snowflake sweater by eight o'clock Tuesday morning. Given

Lena's anxiety about having her stitches removed, Will took a short break from his rounds to be with her. Dr. Jarrett clipped each stitch, and Lena was greatly relieved to feel only a slight tugging sensation as each stitch was removed. A nurse smoothed ointment onto her feet, wrapped them, and placed a blue orthopedic boot with Velcro straps on each of her feet.

Dr. Jarret placed a walker in front of Lena's wheelchair, and a nurse ensured the brakes on the wheelchair were locked. Will helped Lena to her feet. Though she was shaking, more from relief than from fear, he released his grip on her waist and placed Lena's hands on the handle grips of the walker. Lena's first few steps were tentative. Using her arms to bear some of her weight, she slowly made her way around the bed and then to the leather reclining chair. She smiled triumphantly at Dr. Jarrett, who agreed she would be released after physical and occupational therapy.

While Lena was waiting to be discharged after her therapy session that afternoon, she received a call from Gwyn. Aunt Becky and Gwyn had an appointment scheduled with an attorney to look over the legal documents, but Aunt Becky insisted she wanted none of the money. Becky's intention was to give her portion of the money to her two nieces. She was certain Uncle Billy would have wanted her to do so.

Given the dangerously high crime rate in Cordele and faced with the prospect of living alone, Becky wanted Gwyn and Lena to help her relocate to an independent living community for seniors in Colorado. With a modest monthly allowance from Lena and Gwyn to supplement her retirement income, Aunt Becky felt she would be financially comfortable. Her nieces were Becky's last remaining family members, so she wanted to spend her senior years nearby.

While waiting for discharge Lena showed Will the video clips that Jasmyn had captured. He was baffled and suggested he would enjoy a tour of the castle, but preferably during daylight hours. His father had taken him inside the castle once when he was a young boy, but he did not remember anything except for the knight in the foyer.

It was dinner time when Will and Lena pulled up to the carriage house. The short walk from the car to the front door via walker was more tedious and exhausting for Lena than she anticipated. Fatigued, Lena was grateful for the change of scenery and Ria's simple meal of creamed tuna on toast. That night she nestled in the warmth and comfort of Will's arms and slept soundly for the first time in more than a week.

She awoke refreshed and clear-headed, ready to engage in the conversations and decisions that awaited her. Will brought her a cup of coffee and headed toward the bathroom to shower. "Wait," Lena said quietly. "What about me? Don't you think the best way to make sure I don't fall in the shower would be to shower together?"

"Hmmm… that could make my commitment to keep things strictly platonic exceptionally difficult to honor, Ms. Thomas" Will replied.

"Platonic is boring, Dr. Winslow." Lena pulled the blankets down on the bed next to her and patted the mattress. Will obliged, and *eventually* he did help her to shower.

After Will left for work Ria decided to make grilled pancetta, tomato, basil, and mozzarella sandwiches for Lena and herself. Seated on the bench seat in the kitchen breakfast nook with her feet elevated while Ria cooked, Lena texted Gwyn to confirm the video conference she had arranged for the three women at 12:30 p.m. Mountain Standard Time.

Lena dunked her sandwich into the balsamic reduction, bit into the gooey goodness of the sandwich and closed her eyes. "Wow! This is a million times better than those hospital grilled cheese sandwiches!" Lena pondered how strange it must be for Ria to have Lena in her home. "Ria, thank you for lunch, and for allowing me to stay here with you until Gwyn can get back here. I'm grateful, and I can only imagine how awkward it is for you given the situation."

Ria placed a hand on Lena's shoulder and looked at her seriously. "Lena, this is not awkward for me at all. In fact, if I am completely honest, I am thrilled with the situation and excited about my future for the first time since James died. Once Gwyn is on the video conference, I will explain why. In the meantime, tell me about Will! He's accomplished and good looking – what else is there to know?"

"Well, for starters, he is Calvin's son" Lena said, noting Ria's surprised expression. Ria said she had met Calvin's wife once. She was a petite, energetic strawberry blonde. A well-regarded interior designer in Colorado Springs, Mrs. Winslow had helped select finishes and decorate the carriage house for James and herself just before their wedding.

Lena told Ria about her interactions with Will over the past week and a half and described the instant connection she felt with him. While Ria cleaned the dishes, Lena confessed that she felt more comfortable with Will than she had ever felt with a man, which was at odds with her long-held determination to remain single and independent.

Ria smiled knowingly as she placed two cushions from the kitchen barstools under Lena's feet. "I felt that way with James. That feeling is not something you should run from, Lena. It is something you should treasure. You can still be a strong, accomplished woman and also be in love." Ria gave Lena an encouraging wink and settled back into her chair while Lena opened her laptop and clicked on the video conference link.

Gwyn and Becky joined, and Ria started the conversation by explaining that Glen Eyrie had been particularly important to James' father as a descendant of General Panton, and thus also to James, but that she had never been completely comfortable there. The responsibility of ensuring that the castle was preserved and used for purposes aligned with the family's values was important to Ria, but it had been a significant source of stress for her since James' death.

The size of the estate, in Ria's judgment, was substantial enough to ensure that she, Melissa, her grandchildren, Gwyn, Lena, and Becky could all live comfortably if it were split between them. Ria stated firmly that this was something to which Gwyn, Lena, and their Uncle Billy were legally and ethically entitled to, not an act of charity or guilt.

"An equitable share of the estate is your birthright as much as it was James' birthright. It would bring me great comfort if we could agree to preserve the castle and come to an agreement regarding how the property should be used so that I can sell it to you. The $30 million selling price I am offering to you if we can agree on the future use of the property is $12 million below the value at which it was assessed just last week."

Ria paused and looked at the wedding ring she still wore on her left hand. "Knowing that the Glen Eyrie estate remains in the hands of family, knowing that the castle is being preserved and used for good purposes would enable me to move to Japan free from the burden that, in all honesty, the castle currently represents for me."

For two hours the women talked about ideas for the property. They agreed to spend some time discerning and documenting their best ideas, and to talk again in person after Gwyn returned to Colorado Springs. Gwyn thought that would most likely be Saturday morning since her flight did not arrive until late Friday night. After ending the call Lena had just enough time to freshen up before her appointment with Jonathan Stevens.

Ding dong. Ria was helping Lena get comfortable at the dining table when Jonathan arrived. She showed him to the dining room and told Lena she was going to run some errands so the two could have a private meeting.

"Nice to meet you Mrs. Panton" Jonathan said. "May I inquire what you charge for tours of the castle? The way the staff is dressed up has piqued my interest. I'd really like to experience a tour before I leave."

"We don't give public tours, Mr. Stevens, but I'd be happy to show you around." Ria smiled politely.

"Oh – I apologize. The folks standing out in front of the castle when I pulled up led me to the wrong assumption" Jonathan said. "The old-fashioned maid and butler costumes are quaint, and the woman in the long blue dress and the guy in the brown suit look like they jumped straight out of the pages of a history book!"

"Oh, them…" Ria stammered, glancing nervously at Lena. "They will be gone by the time your meeting is finished. I'll be back in half an hour and would be pleased to offer you a private tour before you leave." Ria grabbed her keys and purse from the table in the entryway and waved goodbye.

Jonathan looked over the agreement for the transfer of funds and, finding nothing of concern, encouraged Lena to sign it. He agreed to scan a copy for his records and Lena's, and to have the original couriered to Ria's attorney the following day. Jonathan recommended a detailed addendum to the sale agreement, which would specify the agreement regarding the future use of the property. This would protect Lena and Gwyn, but also document things in such a manner that Ria would likely appreciate. Once an agreement was reached, Jonathan said the addendum was a simple document which he could draw up quickly.

"Lena, can I take off my lawyer hat for a moment and speak to you as your friend?" Jonathan asked. Lena nodded. "You are set for life. You do not need to work anymore – that is, unless you want to. Do you think you will resign from Chamberlain International Realty?"

Lena shook her head. "I've got to get back on my feet, literally, before I think about that. The past week and a half has been emotionally overwhelming and physically very difficult. I will say, though, I have wondered whether purchasing a fair amount of Chamberlain International Realty stock might be a good investment." Jonathan nodded, and affirmed the company's stock was continuing to perform well.

Jonathan gave Lena a gift certificate for a manicure at the Broadmoor and wished her a speedy recovery. When Ria returned, she and Jonathan helped Lena to the guest room so she could rest. Ria ensured the brakes on the walker were set and positioned it next to the bed, well within Lena's reach. Through the guest room window Lena watched Jonathan and Ria walk to the castle's main entrance and disappear through the arched wooden doorway.

She awoke several hours later to the heavy smell of garlic in the air. She went to the guest bathroom to freshen up, surprised that it was after 7:30 p.m. Resenting the necessity of the walker, Lena slowly made her way to the living room where she found Ria wrapped in a large quilt watching television.

She was about to ask Ria what smelled so heavenly when Will entered the room. Still in his blue scrubs, he had a dish towel over his left shoulder and was wearing Ria's floral ruffled bib apron. An amused expression swept over Lena's face.

"Hello, sleeping beauty" Will said with a grin. "I was just about to wake you up for dinner!" Lena tried not to laugh at the sight of Will, but a snicker from Ria soon had both women laughing.

"What's so funny?" Will asked with a confused expression.

"You're... you're just so pretty in your pink feminine apron!" Lena said, still trying not to laugh.

Will looked down and realized he had forgotten to remove the borrowed apron. He looked self-consciously at the two women and shrugged. "Looks like I forgot to take that off! Oh, well. I am perfectly comfortable with my femininity!" He gave Lena a kiss then took her walker, swept her into his arms, and carried her to the candle lit kitchen.

Will placed Lena in a chair at the kitchen table, then pulled Ria's chair out for her. He removed the apron and joined the two women at the table. "Tonight, lovely ladies, I have made for you my world-famous bachelor lasagna, previously frozen garlic bread, and a salad from a bag. It should pair nicely with this lovely Chianti Classico. I hope you will find it to your liking."

Savoring a bite of lasagna, Ria pointed her fork at Lena. "Listen up, cousin! This man is educated, handsome, witty, and a great cook. He is also *really* comfortable with his femininity. I think he's a keeper!"

"Very impressive, Will. This lasagna is fantastic, and I was starving. You're a good cook!" Lena squeezed Will's hand. "Perhaps you are a keeper."

Lena's back was hurting, which she believed was due to constantly sitting or being slightly bent over the walker. She hoped the therapists at her appointment the following morning would allow her to transition from the walker to crutches so she could at least stand up straight. Wide awake thanks to her lengthy afternoon nap, Lena enjoyed talking with Will by the fire until the early hours of the morning.

Lena learned that Will had been engaged eight years prior. His fiancé, Sarah, had been a history professor at the Air Force Academy. She was killed by a drunk driver who ran a red light and broad-sided her car. A young resident on duty in the emergency room at the time, Will had been working when the ambulance brought her in. Sarah was brain dead, and her parents turned off life support the following day. He had dated since Sarah's death, but had not found a meaningful connection. He felt most of the women he met were more interested in his money or the idea of being married to a doctor than they were in him.

Will's best friend, Malcom, lived in Colorado Springs and worked as the chief operations officer for the Broadmoor Hotel and Resort. Malcom was divorced, the result of his ex-wife's affair with a player from the Colorado Avalanche hockey team. Will figured Malcom and Gwyn might have some things in common and suggested they could introduce them.

Lena told Will about her upbringing and her career. She shared that she had been deeply in love with a classmate in college, but the young man's parents were uncomfortable with him dating a woman from "the poor side of the tracks." The young man's parents had threatened to disown him if he continued the relationship. That was when Lena decided that being single would be easiest for her; she had chosen to focus instead on her career. She had already told Will about her relation to General Panton and that she was to receive some inheritance, but she had not yet told him exactly how much she stood to inherit.

"Will, since we are sharing things openly, there is something important I haven't told you." She removed his arm from around her shoulder, sat up and faced him. Money could certainly complicate things, she knew, and Lena did not want to open herself up for being taken advantage of. But Will was comfortable, and she knew she was falling in love.

"That's one serious look on that beautiful face of yours," he said softly as he reached out and stroked her cheek. "I have been completely honest with you and I'd like to pursue a relationship with you, Lena. But honesty and trust are important in a relationship, so if there is something you think I should know, I hope you will trust me enough to be honest with me."

Drawing in a deep breath, Lena decided to be mostly honest as a starting point. "The money I am going to inherit, Will… it is a lot of money."

"Lena, you don't have to tell me anything more. Your financial affairs are your business. I took interest in a gorgeous, ridiculously intelligent real estate agent with frostbite. I have enough money of my own." Will smiled reassuringly and tried to pull her close, but Lena pulled back.

"It is millions" Lena whispered. Will raised his eyebrows, and then put his finger to her lips. She pulled his hand away and continued. "Tens of millions."

Will looked at her in disbelief, then he leaned forward and told her that she should consider consulting privately with a reputable wealth management advisor. Lena agreed, and said Jonathan had given her similar advice and two referrals to people he knew. She yawned, then promised to schedule an appointment with a reputable financial advisor soon. Will carried her to the guest room and laid her gently in the bed.

High-pitched barks and yips from nearby coyotes awakened Lena just before sunrise. As she sat up a wave of painful muscle spasms in her back nearly took her breath away. She slipped quietly out of bed, pulling herself up with the side of her walker, and slowly made her way in the darkness to the living room. Once there she used the walker and coffee table to lower herself to the floor, then laid on her back.

Squeezing her eyes shut, Lena hugged her knees to her chest in an attempt to stretch the muscles in her back. As she straightened herself back out the sound of horses approaching from the distance caused her to open her eyes. Seconds later the sound of Will's alarm from the guest room silenced the horses, and the light in the guest bedroom turned on.

"Oh, God! Lena, baby, you ok?" The sight of Lena laying on the floor alarmed Will, who ran to her side.

"Yes, I'm okay" Lena said, placing a hand on Will's forearm. "Just having some muscle spasms in my back, so I'm stretching."

The hall light turned on and Ria emerged. Seeing Lena on the floor, she hurried to them. Will assured Ria that Lena was alright.

"Did you hear the horses?" Ria asked as she seated herself on the fire-place hearth. Will nodded. While he helped Lena through a series of stretches Ria explained that while there were no horses at the Glen Eyrie estate, she heard them frequently.

No sooner had she spoken the words than the faint sound of running horses approaching caused them to freeze. The horses approached rapidly, then slowed as the sound of hooves on bare earth echoed through the entry way of the carriage house and into the living room. Certain she would be trampled Lena instinctively covered her head with her arms and Will covered her body with his, but the sound stopped just inches from the couple.

Familiar scents of hay and sweaty horses filled the room. Will and Lena could feel the warm, heavy breath of a horse directly above them. Lena opened her eyes, and though she could smell and feel a horse's breath mere inches from her face, she could see nothing. The invisible horse drew in a deep breath, then let out a heavy, audible exhalation.

Will's alarm again sounded from the guest bedroom, and the ghostly sounds and smells of horses vanished. Ria and Will helped Lena up, and the three sat in stunned silence. After confirming with one another what they had experienced, Ria retrieved a heating pad for Lena's back and went to the kitchen to make coffee. Kahlua was a welcomed addition to the morning coffee for all three of them.

Will went to the guest room to shower and dress for work while Lena and Ria chatted by the warmth of the fire. Converting the original carriage house to a residence was the reason Ria believed the ghost horses wandered from time to time, though she had never heard them inside the carriage house before. Lena wondered aloud whether building a small barn and having horses on the property might settle the restless ghost horses.

Though she had never ridden a horse, Lena had been fascinated by the beauty of palomino horses since she was a child. Ria encouraged Lena to learn to ride a horse when she was able and described horseback riding on the Glen Eyrie property as a soul-soothing experience, especially during the fall when the aspen turned gold and the air was crisp. While Ria started laundry and got started on her day, Lena researched local horseback riding instructors.

After his Thursday morning half shift at the hospital, Will returned to the carriage house to pick up Lena for her follow-up appointment at the hospital. Per Will's instructions, Ria had washed new white cotton socks in bleach and placed them in a plastic baggie along with some personal items from the guest bathroom. Will told Lena he had a couple of surprises in store for her after her therapy appointment, but he refused to give her any clues.

While Lena saw the physical and occupational therapist Will waited in the lobby. The therapists taught Lena to walk with crutches, which they wanted her to use for five days. After that they believed she would be comfortable bearing full weight on her feet. The physical therapist told Lena she could stop wearing the orthopedic shoes and transition to clean tennis shoes with good support and tread provided she also wore clean cotton socks.

When Lena hobbled into the lobby, she found Will asleep in a chair. She realized he had either been working at the hospital or tending to her for several days. She tapped his calf gently with a crutch. Will opened his eyes to see Lena standing straight, beaming from ear to ear.

"Hey, good looking!" Lena said. "I need to buy some good tennis shoes. Will you take me shopping, please?"

Will rubbed his eyes, then looked at his watch as he stood up. "Yes, we have time to find some shoes before our appointment, and I know just the right place." On the way to the shoe store Lena begged Will to tell her what the surprise was, but he refused. He bought her several pairs of socks and a pair of athletic shoes with good arch support and enough tread to provide good traction in case it snowed again.

Then he took her to the Broadmoor hotel, where the valet greeted them with a wheelchair. Will wheeled her to the hotel's five-star spa, where he had arranged deep tissue massages for them in the couples' suite. As Lena's back muscles slowly surrendered to the masseuse's hands, she marveled at what a perfect and thoughtful surprise Will had arranged. After their massage, Will said there was one more surprise in store for Lena and left to shower and change.

A few moments later a woman from *The Boutique at the Broadmoor* arrived in the couple's suite with a rack of outfits for Lena to choose from. She also handed Lena a bag containing her makeup, deodorant, and other personal items. In the women's changing room Lena donned her new Eileen Fisher pants and sweater, which she thought looked a bit strange with her new white and silver tennis shoes.

Will was waiting for her in the spa lobby, looking handsome in pressed slim fit slacks and a fitted white collared shirt. He was standing next to a man who he introduced as his friend Malcom. The hotel kept a scooter on hand for injured guests, which Malcolm had arranged for Lena to borrow. With Lena following on the scooter, Malcom carried her crutches as he led the way to a private dining room.

"Lena, so nice to meet you" Malcom said as Will helped Lena from the scooter to a chair at a tapestry-draped table for two set with ivory and gold china. "I hope you will enjoy the meal our head chef has prepared for you. To celebrate your recovery and that goofy grin that you have put on Will's face, the wine is on me tonight. I recommend the Catena Zapata Adrianna Vineyard Malbec. It is a great bold wine from Argentina that will be a nice compliment to your meal."

Lena agreed, and Malcom left her and Will to enjoy their private dinner date. The four-course meal the couple enjoyed was one of the finest Lena had ever experienced. She shared with Will that she was confident neither of her parents had ever enjoyed such a fancy meal. Will, who had enjoyed a relatively privileged upbringing, grew up having annual birthday brunches at the Broadmoor, so it was an establishment that held fond memories for him. Over dessert, a decadent hazelnut Mille Feuille with a rich port, Will grew quiet.

"Will, is everything alright?" Lena asked.

Will savored a sip of port and leaned back in his chair. "Gwyn will be here Saturday, Lena. You are getting around fairly well, and I know you'll head back to Denver at some point soon." He set his glass on the table and met her eyes. "I have treasured every moment with you, Lena Thomas. I know the distance between Denver and Colorado Springs is something we would have to figure out, but I would like to date you exclusively. I'm hoping you might feel the same way."

Lena smiled and reached across the table for Will's hand. She had not told him yet that she planned to purchase the castle at Glen Eyrie. "I do feel the same way, Will. I am not sure exactly what the immediate future looks like for me, but I do know I'll be spending a lot of time in Colorado Springs. Dating you exclusively sounds wonderful."

Smiling, Will pulled a small red gift bag from under his chair and slid it across the table to her. Lena opened the bag, which contained a key taped to Will's business card. On the back of the business card was a handwritten address and a five-digit code.

"That is a key to my house, and the access code to the garage. It is not as nice as Ria's place by any means, but it is not full of spirits, either. Since we have already broken our pact about keeping things platonic, I would also like to point out that my place also offers more privacy." He shot her a winning smile. "No pressure. Just know that I would love to have you stay with me anytime – that is, if you are comfortable with the idea."

Lena took her napkin off her lap and set it to the left of her plate. Then she leaned forward and whispered mischievously, "Is tonight too soon?"

Chapter Thirteen Recipes

Cream Tuna on Toast

½ stick butter
1 c. milk
¼ c. flour
1 can tuna, drained
Salt and pepper to taste
Toast

Directions:

1. Melt butter in a saucepan over medium-high heat.

2. Add milk and flour. Stir with whisk until thick.

3. Add tuna, salt, and pepper.

4. Spoon over toast and enjoy.

Will's Bachelor Lasagna

1 lb. sweet Italian sausage, browned and drained
6 oz. sliced pepperoni
1 box oven ready lasagna noodles
Fresh basil leaves, sliced into thin strips (¼")
2 24 oz. jars pasta sauce
¼ c. red wine
1 T. cocoa powder (yes, really!)
2 T. Penzey's Tuscan Sunset Italian Seasoning
1 t. garlic salt
¼ c. water
2 c. shredded mozzarella cheese
2 c. shredded parmesan cheese
8 slices Velveeta cheese

Directions:

1. Brown ground sausage and drain.

2. Combine pasta sauce, wine, cocoa, Tuscan Sunset, and garlic salt. Stir well.

3. Spray a 9x13" casserole dish with cooking spray and add water to the dish.

4. Cover bottom of dish with lasagna noodles, breaking some noodles as needed to provide a consistent layer.

5. Ladle one-third of the sauce mixture over the noodles and spread evenly.

6. Top sauce with ½ of the browned Italian sausage.

7. Cover meat with 1 c. shredded mozzarella and 1 c. shredded parmesan.

8. Cover cheese with lasagna noodles, breaking some noodles as needed to provide a consistent layer.

9. Ladle one-third of the sauce mixture over the noodles and spread evenly.

10. Top sauce with sliced fresh basil.

11. Top basil with Velveeta slices.

12. Cover cheese with lasagna noodles, breaking some noodles as needed to provide a consistent layer.

13. Ladle one-third of the sauce mixture over the noodles and spread evenly.

14. Top sauce with remaining Italian sausage.

15. Cover meat with 1 c. shredded mozzarella and 1 c. shredded parmesan.

16. Bake at 350 degrees for 45 minutes or until cheese is melted and begins to brown.

— CHAPTER 14 —

Scattered Words

Pain in Lena's feet woke her shortly after 4:00 a.m. Because of the unplanned stay at Will's place, she had not had access to pain medication since lunch time the previous day. Uncomfortable and certain she would not be able to go back to sleep, she decided to get up and try to find something in Will's medicine cabinet to help with the pain. She sat up and reached for Will's dress shirt, which lay crumpled on the floor. She put it on, then reached for her crutches, and stood up slowly.

"Can't sleep, pretty lady?" Will asked sleepily.

"No, I can't sleep. My feet hurt. You were right about staying on top of the pain by taking the medication on schedule, but I left it at Ria's place." She smiled as she admired the silhouette of Will's naked body in the dimly lit room. "I'll scare up some coffee and take care of myself, Will. You should get some rest. You've done nothing but work and cater to me for days."

Will sat up and stretched. "Catering to you has been my pleasure." He stood up and strode to a dresser, then leaned down and removed a pair of sweatpants from the drawer. "Besides," he said, pulling the sweatpants over his bare back side, "I was already awake just watching you sleep. Let's have some coffee and toast, then I'll take you back to Ria's."

Will headed to the kitchen, and Lena went to the bathroom to freshen up. Then she crutched her way to the living room and settled into a black leather reclining loveseat. Will had turned on the gas fireplace and set up two large cushions for Lena's feet. He entered the room with a cup of water and several ibuprofen tablets, which Lena accepted gratefully. She pulled a heavy hand knit afghan from the back of the couch.

Will re-emerged from the kitchen with two cups of coffee in hand. "My mom knit that blanket for me when I left for college." He kissed her softly then handed her a cup of coffee. "I love having you in my house, Lena Thomas, and I *really* dig your outfit! It sure would be a shame if you decided to cover it up with a blanket."

Aware that she was wearing only her panties and Will's dress shirt, Lena shrugged casually. "You know, Mr. Winslow, I like waking up with you. I like it so much that I will share the warmth of this special blanket with you." He sat next to her and draped his right arm over her shoulder. "Will, I have to say that last night was the most incredible date I have ever been on. To be honest, I have been feeling pretty down since being hospitalized, so thank you for surprising me with an unforgettable evening. You know, I could get used to being spoiled like that!"

Will reached over and tucked Lena's hair behind her left ear. "I had a fantastic evening, too, but I feel badly. Look, Lena, one of the things we have in common is busy, active lifestyles. It makes sense that your feet hurt from not taking your meds on schedule, and to be honest the evening was probably a bit much given your situation. I respect your independence, Lena, I really do. But will you please promise me that you will take it easy today at Ria's house? It would be smart to keep your feet elevated and let your body rest until Gwyn gets back tomorrow."

Lena smiled and rested her hand on Will's knee. "Yes, I promise. But if I had a choice, I would much rather spend the day right here with you, Dr. Winslow." Lena watched the flames dance in the fireplace as she contemplated what her parents would think of Will. Maybe the stealth focus on her career need not be such a priority going forward given her inheritance, she thought. If she were to scale back her real estate work, perhaps focusing on investments and special properties of historical significance, it would free up time for Lena to invest in a relationship with Will.

As if reading her mind Will said, "I wish you could have met my mom, Lena. I think the two of you would have gotten along well." He squeezed her shoulder, then removed the blanket from his lap and stood up. Stretching, he said, "Let me catch a quick shower and put on some scrubs, then I'll drive you back to Ria's. Want to borrow some sweatpants?"

Lena eyes Will mischievously. "Mmm hmm. Yep. I want *those* sweats," she said, tugging at Will's waistline.

"More than happy to oblige, ma'am. But *these* sweatpants come at a price!" Will said slyly as he dropped his pants to the floor.

It was just after 7 o'clock when Will and Lena arrived at the carriage house, and Ria was still sleeping. Lena showered, then made herself comfortable on Ria's living room sofa. Using the coffee table and cushions from the blue velvet upholstered chairs, Will created a soft perch on which Lena could elevate her achy feet. He handed her the television remote, then went to get a glass of iced water so she could take her pain medication. When he returned, he laid down on the couch with his head in Lena's lap and fell asleep.

Lena had just started to doze off herself when she felt the startling weight of a hand on her knee. Fearing what she might see, Lena pondered briefly whether she should pretend to be sleeping. It was probably Ria, she reasoned. Curiosity got the better of her, so she slowly opened one eye. Appearing completely solid in the morning sunlit room was General Panton. He was bent at the waist with his cane in his left hand, and his right hand rested on her knee. His hazel eyes met hers. Smiling, he said, "Welcome home, Selena. You are my blood, fruit of my secret love. You must preserve my legacy, a legacy with and for others." His voice was warm and soft, and Lena felt oddly comforted by his presence.

"I will, grandfather" Lena whispered softly. "I promise." The General stood up straight and smiled. Then he nodded, turned, and slowly drifted out of the room. Lena watched as the man passed Ria, who stood in the hallway in her bathrobe with a shocked expression on her face. General Panton, seemingly oblivious to Ria's presence, continued through the entry hallway and walked straight through the closed carriage house front door.

Seemingly frozen with her mouth agape, Ria stared at the front door for several seconds. Lena reached out to Ria with her hand. Perhaps because she was psychologically numb from the pain medication, or perhaps because she did not wish to awaken Will, Lena was surprisingly calm.

"You saw him, right? The General?" Lena asked in a hushed voice as Ria's hand reached her own. Ria perched herself on the coffee table facing Lena and nodded.

"Yes, I did." Ria whispered. "For your sake, Lena, I really hope the spirits start to settle down now that the family secrets have been revealed. As for me, damn it, I just do not have the mental fortitude to handle seeing them. For right now this is still *my* house – they could at least have the decency to knock!" Ria glanced over her shoulder at the front door, then back at Lena.

Lena offered a half-hearted smile. "They startle me, too, but the horse spirit is the only one that still scares me. You know, if you had told me two weeks ago that I would be having a conversation with you about ghosts I would have laughed in your face. This whole situation really has been so… unbelievable. The truth is that I never really considered the possibility that our essence can exist beyond this lifetime."

Ria drew in a deep breath and sighed. "I suppose there is some comfort in knowing that we don't just cease to exist when we pass away. And it is also comforting to know that our loved ones can apparently keep watch over us, or at least check in on us from time to time."

Looking down at Will, who was still asleep with his head in Lena's lap, Ria said, "You must be tired – it appears the two of you had a long night. Want to tell me about it?" Ria raised her eyebrows and shot Lena a knowing smirk.

Lena nodded in acknowledgment and grinned sheepishly. "We had a great night, Ria. He took me to the Broadmoor for a massage and dinner in a private dining room. I promise to tell you about it later" Lena said, noting the heat in her flushing cheeks. "But to be honest pain in my feet has had me awake since four o'clock, and I am pretty wiped out. My eyelids are calling."

"Okay then. But you are not off the hook – I expect to hear all about it when you wake up." Ria formed her thumb and index finger into a circle, and held her other fingers straight, giving Lena the OK sign as she headed to the kitchen. Lena looked down at Will, who was still sleeping soundly.

She turned off the television, rested her hand gently on Will's shoulder, and watched him sleep.

A legacy for and with others. The General's words echoed through Lena's mind. She knew the General's philanthropic efforts had been more than helping freed slaves after the end of World War II. The General had valued education highly. He had built a school for the deaf and blind and a hospital for tuberculosis patients. It occurred to Lena that the General's legacy was about contributing to the common good by serving the poor and the marginalized. Perhaps, Lena thought, the rampant racial and political division in contemporary society could be mitigated by a similar, albeit more modern approach to the General's legacy.

A brief, faint breeze in the room caught Lena's attention, followed by the faintest scent of Charlie perfume. Lena knew that her mother was near, though she could see nothing out of the ordinary. Comforted by the thought of her mother and overwhelmed by the potent combination of fatigue and pain medication, Lena closed her eyes and drifted to sleep.

She dreamt that she was walking toward the aspen grove. When she arrived at the clearing, she noticed several words scattered on the ground, rustling gently in the breeze as if they might be autumn leaves. Lena bent down to touch the words, which seemed to be rearranging themselves, but a rustling in the trees caused her to shift her gaze. On the edge of the clearing stood General Panton with her mother; both figures held a bundle of red Indian paintbrush flowers in their hands. Though no words were spoken, in her dream state Lena understood an important connection between the General's philanthropic contributions and the words her mother's spirit had spoken to her several days before in the hospital.

Change hearts and lives, my Lena. Be wise with your blessings. The sound of her mother's voice and the warm breath in her left ear caused Lena to awaken with a start and a loud gasp. Confused by the palpable sensation of warm breath on her ear and certain that she had just heard her mother's voice, Lena blinked her eyes in disbelief. A desperate sense of longing for her mother clutched at Lena's heart, and she knew she was helpless to stop the tears that welled instantly in her eyes.

"Lena are you alright?" Ria asked with concern as she entered the room carrying a tray of meat, cheese, and crackers. "Will left for work a while ago and... Oh, sweetie, you are crying. What's the matter?" Ria set the tray on the coffee table and reached for a box of tissues, which she handed to Lena.

Lena smiled slightly as she accepted the tissues and wiped the tears from her face. "Yes, I am okay. Just a really vivid dream. My mom was there, and so was the General. And there were words on the ground..." Lena's mind raced as she struggled to recall the words that had been scattered on the ground in her dream. "Ria, would you mind handing me a pen and a piece of paper?"

From a drawer in the side table next to the couch Ria removed a black felt tip pen and a pad of yellow post-it notes, which she handed to Lena. Scribbling words on four separate post-it notes as quickly as she could, Lena's mind raced. *Philanthropy. Panton. Common Good. Thomas.* She got up from the couch and knelt on her knees in front of the coffee table, where she rearranged the words for several moments until they made sense to her. Ria sat on the couch and watched, curious about what Lena was doing. There was an intensity, perhaps even a desperateness in Lena's focus.

When Lena finally stopped moving the post-it notes around, she turned around and looked at Ria with an expression that was simultaneously dumbfounded and relieved. "I know what we need to do with the estate" Lena said quietly. "Ria, do you have time to spare this afternoon? I cannot wait to share with you what I believe we are supposed to do with the estate. It is probably best that you and I figure out some details before Gwyn comes back tomorrow."

Ria helped Lena back to the couch, then turned to face her. "Lena, whatever your idea is, I have a sense that it is the perfect solution. All I can think about – day or night – is leaving this place. I am ready. I want to be with Melissa and her family, and I know this is what James wants for me, too." Ria smiled bravely. "So, let's eat our lunch and then figure out next steps together, ok? More importantly, I want you to know that you are a legitimate and perfect part of the Panton family, Lena. I hope we can stay close always."

— CHAPTER 15 —

An Enduring Legacy

G len Eyrie Castle: A Bed & Breakfast Destination and home of the Panton-Thomas Foundation for Philanthropy and the Common Good. With the signage up and the 501(c)(3) nonprofit status secured Ria, Gwyn and Lena spent several weeks building a board. Ria agreed to chair the Panton-Thomas Foundation board, which would bring together wealthy Colorado philanthropists to fund community initiatives focused on equity and inclusion for poor and marginalized persons in Colorado. Within weeks of agreeing on the idea, Ria, Lena, and Gwyn had secured commitments from a diverse membership of more than 30 people representing journalism, education, entertainment, non-profits, politics, finance, law, business, religion, recreation, mental health, government, and agricultural interests.

David agreed to be a founding member on the Board and was helpful in recruiting several high-profile friends and associates to also join the Foundation board. Will would represent the medical community, Malcolm agreed to represent hospitality and tourism, Gwyn agreed to represent the food and beverage industry, and Lena would represent the real estate industry.

Ria relocated to Japan and was thoroughly enjoying the opportunity to explore a new culture and spend time with her daughter, son-in-law, and grandchildren. Aunt Becky moved into an independent living apartment at Liberty Heights Assisted Living in Colorado Springs. Becky cherished spending time with her nieces. Gwyn had become exceedingly popular with Aunt Becky's neighbors for bringing tasty treats when she visited.

After the purchase of the castle was complete Gwyn and Lena made several changes in their own lives. Lena lived with Will at his home while the carriage house was updated and redecorated. After their wedding Will and Lena made the carriage house their permanent residence. Gwyn quit her job in Denver and moved to Colorado Springs. She and Malcolm were engaged and living together in the castle.

The sisters had a rustic stone barn built behind the castle, and three acres were fenced off with a stone fence that matched the red stone of Glen Eyrie castle. Calvin supervised the construction and taught Gwyn and Lena to ride and agreed to move into the apartment above the barn in exchange for occasional handyman work and care for the horses and tack. The barn was the perfect location for the new horses, four of which were palominos named Willie, Queenie, Mitilde, and Charlie. Guests of the castle could enjoy horse riding lessons and trail rides through the wooded trails on the property. Lena ensured that the old schoolhouse at Glen Eyrie retained its historic charm and character as it was updated to serve as a technology-enabled meeting space for the Panton-Thomas Foundation, though the aging painted exterior was replaced with rustic wood siding.

The well-publicized grand opening for Glen Eyrie Castle was to be a fundraiser for the Panton-Thomas Foundation. The black-tie gala would include dinner, dancing, celebrity guests, and a silent auction. The invitations promised guests a private performance of David's soon-to-be-released single, *Spirit*, if the fundraising goal of $2 million for the event was reached.

Melissa and Ria flew to Colorado from Japan for the gala. Both women were thrilled with the plans for Glen Eyrie and with the updates to the property. Jasmyn had graduated from college and was in the process of relocating to Colorado Springs to move in with Dillon. Lena had hired Jasmyn to help open a new Colorado Springs office for Chamberlain International Realty that would focus on historic properties.

On the eve of the gala limousines streamed through the castle gates at Glen Eyrie, their headlights illuminating the showy yellow and gold hues of the autumn aspens. Among the gala guests were the governor of Colorado, several famous recording artists, local news personalities, players from the

Denver Broncos and Denver Nuggets teams, and representatives from the Bill and Melinda Gates Foundation. Jasmyn, who had graduated from college, arrived on Dillon's arm wearing a stunning red sequined gown. Kacie arrived with her new boyfriend, a prominent oncologist from Denver. David, who was serving as emcee for the event in the great hall, was dashing in a wine-colored tuxedo and bowtie made of dollar bills.

With the party well underway waitstaff roamed the ballroom providing appetizers and bartenders ensured that guests did not roam empty-handed. At Ria's queue, David approached the microphone and encouraged the guests to find their seats.

"Dinner will be served momentarily, friends. While our wonderful waitstaff delivers the first course to your tables, I'd like to ask you to help me thank the woman who planned the food for this event. Let's give a warm round of applause to The Panton-Thomas Foundation's executive chef, Ms. Gwyn Thomas." Gwyn stood and offered a polite wave to the crowd.

"Ladies and gentlemen," David continued. "I have an incredible update. This evening we have raised $1,858,000 for the Panton-Thomas Foundation for Philanthropy and the Common Good." David paused as the crowd cheered politely from their dinner tables. "We are just $142,000 from our fundraising goal for the evening. I think there is only one person who can convince you to open your wallets and help us reach that goal. Please help me welcome the visionary behind the Panton-Thomas Foundation and co-owner of Glen Eyrie Castle, Mrs. Lena Thomas-Winslow."

Her growing baby bump shifted as Lena stood and motioned for Ria, Melissa, and Gwyn to accompany her to the stage. Will extended his arm and escorted her to the microphone as the crowd applauded. The lights dimmed as planned, and the projector turned on.

Lena shared with the gala guests the story of General Panton and his legacy of philanthropy to help the poor and the marginalized. She explained his relationship with Mitilde Thomas. Scanned photographs of General Wynston Jamison Panton, Queenie, their daughters, Charles Thomas, Mitilde, and their children progressed as she shared the history. Then a more recent photograph of a young girl in a smocked dress sweeping the floor of a shop appeared on the screen. Next to the girl in the photo was a toddler in a stroller.

Lena reached for Gwyn's hand and pulled her forward. "This is my sister, Gwyn. We were children like the ones we are raising funds for this evening. The picture on the screen is a picture of me when I was seven years old. From the time I was six, I swept the floor of a local bakery in exchange for a loaf of bread because my family was poor, and we had little to eat. An exceedingly kind and generous man named Mr. Gerardy was the owner of that bakery, and I last saw him at my mother's funeral."

"Mr. Gerardy is a big reason for tonight's event." Lena paused a moment to blink back a tear. "You see, every time I thanked Mr. Gerardy for the bread, he reminded me to always share my treasure with those who are less fortunate. And then he would hug me, give me a piece of candy and a loaf of bread, and send me home. He also purchased school supplies for myself and my sister on many occasions. He was always active in our community and hosted annual school supply drives at his bakery that benefitted many kids like Gwyn and me."

"At my mother's funeral I promised Mr. Gerardy that I would honor his generosity by paying it forward someday. I have helped other people along the way, and Mr. Gerardy's guiding voice was always in the back of my mind. But the truth is that the focus of tonight's gala and fundraiser, making college possible for high-risk, high-potential Colorado kids, was inspired by this humble baker from Cordele, Georgia."

"I called Mr. Gerardy recently and told him about how much my life had changed. I wanted him to know that his kindness and advice were one of the most powerful influences in my life. Mr. Gerardy is retired now, but do you know what he did? At the age of 81 Mr. Gerardy flew to Colorado and baked all of the bread for tonight's event. In fact, he is here tonight as my very special guest. Will you please join me in welcoming a man who embodies wisdom, generosity, and service to others, Mr. Ben Gerardy and his lovely wife Bernice."

Mr. Gerardy stood at his table and waived at the applauding crowd. "At this time, I would like to turn the microphone to the chairwoman of the

Panton-Thomas Foundation for Philanthropy and the Common Good, my dear friend Ms. Ria Panton." Ria approached the microphone hand in hand with Melissa. After introducing her daughter, Ria asked that the presentation slide be advanced.

"Mr. Gerardy, it is my pleasure to inform you that the scholarships made possible through this evening's events will be given in your honor. The Board voted unanimously last week to name these scholarships the Ben and Bernice Gerardy Bright Futures Scholarship." The crown rose to its feet and Mr. Gerardy wiped his eyes with his napkin.

Ria continued. "Glen Eyrie castle is a beautiful place and General Panton's legacy must be continued. The board has declared that this fundraising gala will be an annual event focused on a specific area of community need in the Centennial state. Each year we will recognize one person, nominated by the citizens of Colorado, to receive the Wynston Jamison Panton Humanitarian Award. The award will be presented annually at this event to someone whose selflessness, generosity, and commitment to the common good impacts the lives of the less fortunate in powerful ways."

Ria paused and glanced back at Lena before continuing. "Tonight, on behalf of the Panton-Thomas Foundation for Philanthropy and the Common Good, it is my honor and my pleasure to present the first annual Wynston Jamison Panton Humanitarian Award to Mr. Ben Gerardy in appreciation for his years of generosity and selfless service to others." As the crowd rose to its feet, Mr. and Mrs. Gerardy approached the stage. Mr. Gerardy embraced Lena and Gwyn, steadying himself with his cane.

Mr. Gerardy approached the microphone, removed a handkerchief from his worn blue suit, and wiped his eyes as he accepted the engraved glass statue from Ria. "What a nice surprise. Thank you all so much. To be honest I never felt like I ever amounted to much, so it is a gift to know that I impacted someone's life positively. You know, I am not a wealthy man. Never have been. But I always made enough to support my family. Now over the years I reckon Bernice and I have given away hundreds of loaves of bread to people who needed it, and I also reckon that our school drives at the bakery have helped a couple thousand school kids."

The crown applauded again, then Mr. Gerardy continued. "If a simple man like me, a baker from Cordele, Georgia with no high school degree can help other people, then I can't help but wonder what each of you can do. Now based on all the fancy dresses and suits I see out there, I'm pretty sure most of you have the financial means to make a difference. Please, I ask you to open your hearts and your wallets to help these kids get to college if you can afford to help. If even one of these scholarship kids turns out like Lena or Gwyn, then your gift will impact generations of people. Thank you for this award and thank you for sharing your blessings with others." The crowd offered Mr. Gerardy a hearty standing ovation as he and his wife returned to their seats.

David returned to the microphone. "Ladies and gentlemen, the money raised this evening will provide tuition, books, fees, and mentors for first generation high-potential high school seniors in Colorado whose families don't have the financial means to send them to college. So please, pull out that checkbook and help us send these kids to college."

"While you do that, I have a piece of information for you that I'll bet you didn't know. Glen Eyrie Castle is haunted! It's true! Candlelight guided tours of the castle start at 8:30 and depart every ten minutes, so if you have not signed up for a tour yet, this is a good time to do so. Enjoy your dessert, and please consider writing a check to help the Panton-Thomas Foundation reach its fundraising goal. I'll be back by eight o'clock, and then we'll celebrate with music and dancing!"

Sweeping Lena into his arms, Will smiled at his wife. "Lena Thomas-Winslow, I am proud to be your man. You really are something special, and this evening is a huge success. I love you."

"The spirits of Glen Eyrie brought me many gifts. The greatest of those gifts was you, Dr. Winslow. And our son. I can't wait to meet him." Lena smiled at Will as someone tapped on her shoulder.

"Excuse me, Mrs. Winslow?" Lena turned around to see Denver Broncos outside linebacker Vaughn Millner standing next to her. Vaughn extended his hand, which Lena shook firmly. "My name is Vaughn Millner; I play for the Denver Broncos."

"Mr. Millner, I'd be a fool not to recognize you. I am a huge fan – in fact, I have your jersey! Thank you for giving Denver Broncos fans so many reasons to celebrate and thank you for being here tonight."

Vaughn gestured toward the beautiful woman on his arm. "My lovely wife here said I'm not allowed to leave this party unless I make sure that your fundraising goal is reached. This ought to do it." Vaughn handed Lena a check.

Without looking at the check Lena thanked the football great and addressed his wife. "Mrs. Millner, thank you for applying a little pressure. I don't suppose you have time in your busy schedule to join the Panton-Thomas Foundation as a member of the board? We would be honored to have you join us."

Mrs. Millner accepted Lena's invitation, and the two exchanged contact information. As the Millners departed Lena looked at the check, which was written for the amount of $150,000. Blinking back victorious tears, Lena took the check to the accountants in the back of the room who were busy totaling donations for the evening then stepped out into the hall for a moment alone.

Alone in the hall Lena leaned against the wall, closed her eyes, and took a deep breath. "I hope you are proud, mama and grandfather Panton," she whispered softly.

Yes, Selena. You have done well. Thank you. General Panton's voice was soft and close to her ear. Lena opened her eyes. In the far corner of the hallway, she could barely make out the figures of General Panton, Queenie, Mitilde, Charles, and both of her parents.

"Lena, you okay?" Will approached, looking at her with concern. When Lena didn't move or respond, he followed her gaze. "Well, it makes sense that they would attend this event. Haven't seen them for a while."

"Yes, I'm fine. Tired, but happy my love." Lena took Will's hand and the couple headed back to the ballroom. Moments later the lights dimmed, and David headed to the stage. "Ladies and gentlemen, please find your way to your seats. The time has come to reveal whether we have reached our fundraising goal for the evening. I need your help counting down from ten to one. When we finish the countdown, the total amount raised tonight will be displayed on the screen. Are you ready?"

The crowd joined in counting down with David. "10… 9… 8… 7… 6… 5…." Lena stood between Ria and Gwyn squeezing their hands tightly. "4… 3… 2… 1!" The screen turned on; it read $2,442,551.

"Folks, this is tremendous!" David exclaimed. "This money will impact the lives of high-potential Colorado students for the rest of their lives. Thank you!" Gold and silver balloons dropped from the ceiling as the crowd rose to their feet and cheered.

"If you read your invitations, you know that I promised to perform my new single, which is set to be released next week." David pulled off his jacket and bowtie and unbuttoned the top two buttons on his shirt. Whistles from a few tipsy women in the crowd ensued as he strapped on his guitar. The band began to play, and David said, "This song is called 'Spirits.' It was inspired by the generations of spirits who are said to roam the halls here at Glen Eyrie Castle. I hope you like it! Thank you for your generosity – the rest of the evening is for dancing and celebrating!"

David's new song was a hit with the crowd, and the gala guests enjoyed dancing, drinking, and tours of the castle. Finally, at 10:00 the lights dimmed and the band stopped playing, signaling the end of the evening. Ria, David, Lena, and Gwyn stood in the foyer and thanked each guest as they departed.

Many guests expressed appreciation for the wonderful people in period costume they had encountered throughout the evening. One particular man requested an opportunity to thank the butler, who had caught his wife when she tripped over her gown while navigating the stairs. He was certain she would have been severely injured had the butler not been there. Ria told the man that the butler had left for the evening, but that she would pass along the man's gratitude.

When the last of the guests had departed, a few special guests gathered in the main dining hall for a private celebration. Lena tapped her champagne flute of sparkling water once champagne had been poured for the others in the room. "I would like to propose a toast, please. I raise my glass to each of you, and to the spirits of Glen Eyrie. You… and they… have taught me that love, kindness, and generosity will always be victorious against war, injustice, prejudice, and inequity, and I am grateful."

Ria toasted Lena in return, and they enjoyed sharing stories of the evening. As Will and Lena rose to signal the end of the private celebration, the screeching sound of metal scraping against metal emanated from the main reception hall. The party followed Lena and Will through the dining room doorway to the main reception hall. Standing squarely in the middle of the reception hall facing the friends stood the iron knight holding a bundle of bright red Indian paintbrush flowers in its right hand.